His eyes glimmered. 'You still hover on the brink between exasperation and caring for me, don't you? Go on, admit it.'

'I won't. You're a pain in the neck, Connor. You always have been and you'll probably stay that way for ever.'

He put an arm around her shoulders and drew her to him. 'But despite all that you do care for me just a teensy bit, don't you?'

'I'm not admitting to anything. You drive me to distraction.'

'I'll settle for that,' he murmured. 'For the time being at least. Distracted is good. I like distracted.'

Slowly he lowered his head, until his cheek was just a breath away from hers, and then, before Phoebe had time to realise what he was about, he was kissing her softly, tenderly, his lips brushing hers and exploring the curving line of her mouth.

The kiss was like a lick of flame gliding along her nerve-endings. Heat built up in her, engulfing her, taking her over, so that she could think of nothing but the sheer ecstasy of that moment. Everything went out of her head.

Phoebe drew back from Connor, looking at him with bemusement in her eyes.

'Are you okay?' he asked.

'I don't know.' She was floundering, her nervous system firing off sparks as though he had inadvertently lit a fuse in her.

He smiled. 'Shall I kiss you again and see if things come any clearer?'

When **Joanna Neil** discovered Mills & Boon®, her lifelong addiction to reading crystallised into an exciting new career writing Medical™ Romance. Her characters are probably the outcome of her varied lifestyle, which includes working as a clerk, typist, nurse and infant teacher. She enjoys dressmaking and cooking at her Leicestershire home. Her family includes a husband, son and daughter, an exuberant yellow Labrador and two slightly crazed cockatiels. She currently works with a team of tutors at her local education centre to provide creative writing workshops for people interested in exploring their own writing ambitions.

Recent titles by the same author:

THE SURGEON SHE'S BEEN WAITING FOR
CHILDREN'S DOCTOR, SOCIETY BRIDE
HIS VERY SPECIAL BRIDE
PROPOSING TO THE CHILDREN'S DOCTOR
A CONSULTANT BEYOND COMPARE

THE REBEL
AND THE
BABY DOCTOR

BY
JOANNA NEIL

MILLS & BOON®

First published in Great Britain 2009
Large Print edition 2010
Harlequin Mills & Boon Limited,
Eton House, 18-24 Paradise Road,
Richmond, Surrey TW9 1SR

© Joanna Neil 2009

ISBN: 978 0 263 21060 6

Harlequin Mills & Boon policy is to use papers that are
natural, renewable and recyclable products and made
from wood grown in sustainable forests. The logging and
manufacturing process conform to the legal environmental
regulations of the country of origin.

Printed and bound in Great Britain
by CPI Antony Rowe, Chippenham, Wiltshire

THE REBEL
AND THE
BABY DOCTOR

CHAPTER ONE

PHOEBE pulled open the door of the kitchen cupboard and peered inside. 'It looks as though we're left with just cornflakes for breakfast,' she said, studying the empty shelves. Taking down the packet, she gave it a light shake. 'No, scrub that. It's empty.' She pulled a face and added in exasperation, 'Why do you suppose anyone would put an empty packet back in the cupboard?'

'Search me.' Jessica flicked the switch on the kettle and began to rummage through the contents of the fridge. 'Would you believe it, there's no milk, either? I expect we can put that down to Alex, along with the cornflakes.' She ran a hand raggedly through her long brown hair. 'I must have asked him a hundred times to stop swigging it as if we keep a cow in the back garden. But does he ever listen? It's in one ear and straight out the other.'

Phoebe made a wry smile. 'I guess he must have had a huge thirst after the party last night. I must say I thought he looked a bit the worse for wear this morning when I passed him on the stairs.'

'He'll be even more so if I get my hands on him—preferably around his throat, and with a light application of pressure…' Jessica's mouth formed a wicked grimace of intent as she positioned her hands to demonstrate. 'He knows I need my coffee first thing in the morning.' She frowned. 'So where is he now, I wonder.'

Phoebe closed the cupboard door. 'He's in the bathroom, I think, taking a long shower. He said he needs to clear his head for work this morning.'

'Don't we all?' Jessica moved away from the fridge. 'I was all geared up and ready to start work on Mr Kirk's cardiac team, but now the time's actually arrived I'm wondering if it's going to be everything I thought it would be.

I've heard he's very cool, capable and efficient, but I'm not sure I'll be able to match up to his standards. I struggled a bit with some of the cardiology lectures in med school, but I need the experience if I'm to go on to be a GP.'

'You'll be fine,' Phoebe said firmly. 'You're only having doubts because your stomach is empty and your brain is feeling the effects of that. I wonder if there's anything we can rustle up from the freezer? Hash browns, maybe?' She looked doubtful. 'Anyway,' she added, getting to grips with the situation and swivelling around so that her blonde hair swished lightly before settling into place once more on her shoulders, 'I suppose we could settle for black coffee. That would be better than nothing, wouldn't it?'

She lifted down mugs from a shelf and slid them onto the worktop. 'At least that should help to revive us a bit. It was way late when we finally sloped off to bed, last night. I can't imagine what we were thinking, having a party the night before starting a new rotation.'

'That was it, probably.' Jessica grinned. 'A final fling before it's heads down to some serious work again…that, and the fact that we have a new tenant to celebrate.' Her eyes rolled heavenward. 'The landlord must have had me in mind when he sent Connor to us. He's exactly what I would have ordered up for myself if I'd had free rein. He's stunning. Fabulous just doesn't say it. He's a real hunk, don't you think?' Her mouth quirked briefly. 'Long and lean and vital—and those lovely grey eyes that seem as though they see right into your soul.' She sighed. 'What I wouldn't give to get to know him better. You're so lucky, Phoebe, knowing him from way back when.'

'Hmm. Maybe.'

'Maybe? Are you kidding?' Jessica's voice rose an octave. 'How could you possibly keep your hands off him? He's a stud.'

Phoebe had been studying the contents of the freezer, but now she straightened up and turned to look directly at her friend. 'He's okay—he's definitely all that you say, I'll grant you that. But

if you take my advice, you'll watch your step
with him. He always had something of a reputa-
tion when we lived in the same village as teen-
agers. Ask Alex. He was there at the same time.
In fact, they're related—they're cousins.'

'Oh…you're just afraid to live dangerously,'
Jessica said with a dismissive shake of her head.
'He can come and ring my bell any time.'

Phoebe laughed. 'You're a sucker for a hand-
some face and a winsome manner, aren't you?'
She held out a packet of potato waffles. 'How
about these? Do we grill them or put them in the
microwave?'

Jessica's mouth turned down at the corners.
'Neither. I don't think I could stomach them first
thing in the morning.' She frowned, her mind
diverted only briefly. 'Where is our new house-
mate, anyway? I haven't seen sight or sound of
him this morning. The door to his room was
open, but he wasn't in there when I went by.'

Phoebe's blue eyes sparkled. 'You couldn't
resist looking, could you?' She chuckled. 'I've

no idea where he might be. Connor Broughton was always a law unto himself.'

'Do I hear someone taking my name in vain?'

The back door opened and the subject of their discussion walked in, his arms filled with packages. He elbowed his way into the kitchen, shutting the door behind him with a deft flick of his leather-clad foot.

Jessica made a quick intake of breath. 'Is that food I smell? And coffee?' Her nose twitched and her hazel eyes widened as Connor walked over to the table and put the packages down. 'It is, isn't it?' She sniffed the air, going over to him and watching him as he shrugged off his jacket and laid it over the back of a chair.

Phoebe glanced at him. 'We were wondering where you were,' she murmured.

He was everything Jessica had said, and more. His long legs were encased in expensively tailored dark trousers that moulded his hips to perfection, while his immaculate linen shirt, in a deep blue that reflected the colour of his smoky grey-blue eyes, outlined the flat plane of his stomach. He was way too good looking for any woman's peace of mind, Phoebe decided, and he was altogether too much for her to handle this early in the morning, or at any time, come to think of it.

Distracted and unwilling to allow herself to be sucked any further into his magnetic field, Phoebe averted her gaze and busied herself in a search for plates.

Connor had always been trouble with a capital T and the very fact that he had turned up here in Devon, in this sleepy coastal town, was enough to set her nerves jangling.

'I went out for food,' Connor said as he began to open up the brown paper cartons. 'I called in at the bakery down the road on the off chance they were open for business. Luckily they were, so I bought hot pasties, baguettes, croissants and apricot preserve. I wasn't quite sure what to choose so I decided to bring a selection. The cupboards were empty when I glanced through them this morning and I couldn't face starting the day without anything to eat.'

'Me neither.' Jessica's mouth wavered a fraction as she sent him an appealing glance. 'Were you by any chance planning on sharing any of this feast?'

'Of course.' Connor's brows shot up as he returned her gaze. 'I'm hardly going to sit here and scoff this lot all by myself, am I?'

'Oh, I love you.' Jessica flung her arms around him in delight. 'I'm so hungry. You're my salvation. I think I want to have your babies.'

Connor's mouth curved and his eyes danced with glimmering amusement. 'Really?' He hugged her in return. 'That's not an offer I get every day, but it's certainly one worth thinking about. How many did you have in mind?'

'Oh, a dozen or so, I should think,' Jessica answered, with a grin. 'I'll let you know as soon as I've eaten and my head's back to thinking straight.'

'Ah.' He nodded sagely, looking glum. 'That

could put a bit of a damper on things, I expect. There's nothing to beat a good breakfast for getting the world back to normal and allowing you to see things clearly.'

He released her with a resigned sigh, and went to hunt for crockery, but Phoebe had already beaten him to it. 'Here you are,' she said, handing him plates that she had heated in the microwave. 'Take these. You'd better sit down and eat before it all gets cold. You've cheered us up no end by doing this, you know. We were feeling starved, and now we definitely owe you one.'

'You're very welcome.' He sent her a shrewd glance. 'It was the least I could do since I foisted myself on you with hardly any warning. I know it must have come as something of a shock to have a new tenant land among you.'

Phoebe kept her feelings to herself on that score, saying only, 'We knew the landlord wouldn't leave the room empty for long.' She still hadn't managed to work out what he was actually doing here, choosing to share a house with them.

The Connor she knew from way back in their teens would never have opted for a career in medicine, and consequently, when he'd announced that he was travelling to London to start a new life, that had fulfilled all her expectations. He was always skirting danger and living life on the edge. London was full of exciting possibilities for him.

Something had happened along the way, though, causing him to alter course, and here he was, back in their home county, a qualified doctor in his last few months of hospital training as a senior house officer. A sea change had come about, inasmuch as he was now part of a respectable profession, but Phoebe was wary of how deep that change actually went. Was he still a sleeping tiger, dangerously unpredictable and a hazard to her emotional well-being?

He pulled out a chair and seated himself beside Jessica, who was already chomping on a sausage pasty.

'Mmm...mmm...mmm,' Jessica said with a

satisfied groan. 'This is scrumptious—I'm in heaven. It's so tasty, it's wonderful.'

Connor smiled. 'It certainly sounds as though it is.' He inspected the selection of food, as though he was trying to decide what to choose. 'I was a bit surprised to find the cupboards here were bare—do you have some kind of rota for doing the shopping, or is it down to everyone to fend for themselves?'

'We do have a rota,' Phoebe said, coming to sit down at the table opposite him. 'It was Alex's turn to fetch the groceries, but I think he must have been knocked sideways by the news that he didn't get the rotation he wanted. It was all a bit last minute, and he couldn't quite get his head around it.'

'So the groceries were forgotten?' Connor gave a faint smile, then picked up a breakfast baguette and bit into it. 'Knowing Alex, I can see how that might happen. He's always been fine with the big, important things, and you can rely on him wholeheartedly to deal with those, but I expect anything as mundane as shopping could quite easily pass him by.'

He opened up a carton and the wonderful aroma of coffee escaped and wafted on the air, teasing Phoebe's nostrils.

'I thought the senior house officer posts were all decided well in advance,' he said after a moment or two, pushing a polystyrene cup towards her. 'Did things not go to plan?'

She accepted it gratefully and shook her head. 'I'm not sure what happened, really. He had pinned his hopes on working in A and E, but there was a delay in getting back to him, and he was offered a post in Orthopaedics instead. The powers that be said something about another candidate pipping him to the post.'

She was saddened for a second or two, remembering. 'He was disappointed, but I think he made up his mind that perhaps it wouldn't be a bad idea to accept the orthopaedic job after all. I imagine he'll have the chance of doing a stint in Emergency later.'

'Hmm.' Connor watched as she began to munch thoughtfully on a cheese and bacon pasty, and then asked softly, 'So what rotation will you be working on? As I understand things, we'll all be based at Mount View Hospital. That's what makes living here the perfect choice. Apart from the obvious advantage of being close to the sea, it's only a hop and a skip to work from here.'

She glanced at him. 'I guessed that might be why you turned up on our doorstep out of the blue. Though I was surprised you hadn't decided to stay in London.' She took a sip of her coffee and savoured it for a moment. 'I'm starting a six-month stint that covers children's A and E and the neonatal unit.'

'Ah…that explains a lot. I think I see it all now…' His grey gaze meshed with hers, and he nodded, as though her answer had settled a question in his mind. 'You were hoping that you would be working with Alex, weren't you? You always did have a soft spot for him. I remember from years back you were always hankering after him.' He sent her a teasing smile. 'In fact, there was a time when you two were pretty much inseparable, weren't you? I had the impression last night that nothing much had changed on that front.'

A warning glint came into her eyes. 'I wouldn't go there, if I were you. Alex was always a good friend to me, and I owe him a lot. Unlike some, he knew how to tread the straight and narrow.'

'Ouch!' He made an exaggerated movement, jerking back in his chair and gripping his chest as though she had pierced him with a dart. 'That was a low blow, don't you think? We were young then. Things were different.'

'Were they?' From what she had seen at the party last night, nothing much had changed from her perspective. Connor was still the devil-may-care charmer he had always been, and the girls were hanging on to his every word, trying their best to get close to him. And he certainly wasn't putting up any resistance on that score, was he?

'Do I sense some tension here?' Jessica was looking from one to the other, her curiosity pricked.

'Not at all.' Phoebe's expression still held the faint embers of a glower. 'We understand each other perfectly well, Connor and I. He lives his life in a whirl of reckless abandon and answers to no one, while I stick to the well-worn path and try to follow the rules. We get along fine, just as long as we remember who we are and what we're about.'

'Sounds like a mess of trouble to me,' Jessica commented drily. 'Still, I'm with Connor on the Alex front. I've a good mind to eat up everything in sight just to teach the man a lesson.'

'What lesson would that be?' Alex came into the kitchen in bright and breezy fashion, taking everything in at a glance. He was wearing dark trousers and a fresh-looking dove-grey shirt, and he was altogether easy on the eye. His black hair was peaked in spiky fashion, still damp from his shower. Phoebe gave him a beaming smile.

'Hi, gorgeous.' He dropped a light kiss on her forehead. 'Wow, hot food. That looks good.

Where did this come from? Shove over, Phoebe. Make room for a hungry man.'

Phoebe obliged, sliding onto the chair opposite Jessica, and Alex seated himself next to her. 'Connor went out and bought it for us.'

Jessica sent Alex a long look. 'If we had any sense we'd bar you from the kitchen. Do you know, somebody came in here while we were out and emptied the fridge and ransacked the cupboards? Just after you'd gone to the time and expense of restocking them yesterday.'

'Ah…yes, I was going to do something about that,' Alex said sheepishly, even as he eyed up a crusty baguette. 'Only there was this meeting going on at the students' union building, and what with the party and everything else—well, you know how it is.'

Jessica made a disgruntled sniff, and he gave her a disarming smile. 'I'll sort it later, I promise, on my way back from the hospital.'

She nodded, her eyes narrowing on him. 'You'd better,' she said tartly. 'Or else.'

He made a mock wince, and then turned to glance at Connor. 'Is it all right if I help myself? I'll do the same for you some time.'

'Go ahead.' Connor studied Alex. 'I hear you'll be working in Orthopaedics—that's not such a far cry from A and E, is it? Do you think you'll be okay settling for that?'

'Maybe.' Alex made a face. 'It all depends on whether I can manage to get on good terms with the consultant in charge. We've come across one another once or twice before when I was in medical school, and things didn't always go too well.'

He frowned. 'I had my hopes pinned on the A and E job. I need to do a stint in Emergency at some point, but now it's been delayed for a while. I suppose it won't matter too much…I've not made up my mind what kind of specialty I want to follow yet, but at least I have another eighteen months before I need to make the decision. Unlike you… You're in your final year, aren't you? I heard you already had the offer of a job in London when you finish here.'

'That's right…unless I decide to go on and take specialist exams. I'm still thinking things through.' Connor swallowed some of his coffee. 'This last rotation before the summer break is going to be crunch time for me.'

'Where will you actually be working?' Jessica wiped her hands on a piece of kitchen towel and waited expectantly. 'You wouldn't be coming into Cardiac Care alongside me, would you?' she murmured in a hopeful tone, her eyes growing large. But then she was thoughtful for a moment. 'Mind you…that might not be an altogether good move. Some of the more frail female patients might see you and go all aflutter, and that wouldn't do them too much good, would it?'

Connor chuckled. 'I don't know what to make of you, Jess. Are you always like this? You're irrepressible.'

Jessica gave a nonchalant shrug. 'I don't think I am, not really. I just say it how I see it, and, to be fair, I'm not alone in thinking this way. After all, you weren't short of company last night, were you? I'm sure the word must have gone around, because there were a lot more women here than we actually invited. From what I heard, you're the talk of the nurses' home.'

'I'm not sure whether that's a good or bad thing,' Connor returned wryly. 'Anyway, to go back to what you were saying, I'm actually really serious about medicine. I want to work in Accident and Emergency, and I need to cover all aspects of trauma care if I'm going to do that.'

Phoebe sent him a quick glance. 'And has that worked out for you? Is that what you'll be doing?'

He returned her gaze steadily. 'Yes, as things have turned out, I'll be doing a stint in A and E. I put in a late application, so I wasn't too sure whether I stood a chance. There was some debate as to whether they wanted a junior or a senior to fill the vacancy, and in the end they decided that I would fit the bill.'

Phoebe's eyes narrowed on him. Did that mean that he had taken the job Alex had been after? Was that the reason he had landed here in their patch without warning a couple of days ago? But, then, Alex still had plenty of time to do an A and E rotation. It was unfair to resent Connor for getting the placement, though that wouldn't hurt in her attempts to keep her guard up where Connor was concerned.

She decided not to pursue the subject there and then. It wouldn't be pleasant for Alex to hear how Connor had managed to land the job he had wanted.

Connor had always had the world at his fingertips. He'd never had to struggle for anything. Life treated him well, even when he didn't deserve it, and yet Alex, who was sincere and dedicated, had to work doubly hard to achieve anything.

'It's time we were on our way,' Jessica warned, with a glance at her watch. 'I don't want to be late for my induction meeting. Mr Kirk's a stickler for timekeeping. It wouldn't do to start off with a blot on my record.'

Phoebe nodded, and started to load the dishwasher with the plates they had used. 'Are you ready to go, Alex?' she asked. 'I don't think it will turn out to be half as difficult as you're expecting it to be. You were always good with patients in the fracture clinic and you know a couple of the nurses in Ortho. I'm sure they'll help you out.'

'I've a feeling I'll need all the help I can get.' Alex grimaced. 'Ortho's right next to children's A and E, isn't it? Maybe I'll be able to pop my head round the door and say hello—unless they decide to send you straight to Neonatal instead.'

'Yes, I was wondering about that.' Her mouth turned down a fraction. 'I was hoping I could delay the neonatal side of things for a while.' She frowned. 'I really need to get my head around it. I'm not sure I'll be able to cope with all those tiny babies. They're helpless little mites at the best of times, and even more so in Neonatal Intensive Care. I'm just not sure that I'm up to it—I'm not looking forward to it at all.'

Connor was looking at her oddly. 'Do you not know where you'll be? That seems a little strange.'

'Well, yes, it is unusual, I suppose. They've had a lot of staff changes lately, by all accounts, and the consultants were still working things out when I spoke to them last.' She sent him a direct look. 'Anyway, you'll be okay whatever happens. You've worked in A and E before, haven't you? So there shouldn't be too many surprises for you.'

'I've never worked in children's A and E before this. Apparently I'll be covering both adult and paediatric emergencies, but the bulk of my time will be spent with the paediatric side of things.' He returned her gaze steadily, and she stared at him in disbelief. Was he actually saying he was going to be working in the same department as she was?

'Is something wrong?' Connor was looking at her as though he was trying to work out what was going on in her head.

'No, nothing at all,' she said, schooling her expression into one of blank indifference. It wouldn't do to let Connor know that she had any qualms about working with him, would it? It would only serve to give him ammunition and, once armed, he would tease her mercilessly. She would not let him get to her.

CHAPTER TWO

'IT'S all right to hold him, you know? I promise you, he won't break.' The specialist nurse was smiling as she came to stand beside Phoebe.

'But he's so tiny and vulnerable. I just can't get used to the idea that he's dependent on us for his every need. It's such an awesome responsibility.'

Phoebe was struggling to keep her emotions in check as she looked down at the infant in the cot. A whole range of feelings washed over her, threatening to engulf her. This baby was so fragile, so delicate in every way, with fingers no bigger than matchsticks, curled possessively around the ends of her thumbs, and little legs that were bunched up to his abdomen as though he was still enjoying the safety of the womb.

'I think you'll find that they're a lot tougher than we give them credit for. Most babies are born with the instinct to survive. That's why they cry and gasp and struggle to make their needs known.'

'You're probably right, but I'm glad you're here to help me through this, at any rate,' Phoebe said, glancing towards the nurse. 'I have to check him out to see what's causing his problems, but you've probably already diagnosed him on instinct.'

'Sort of. I have my theories. I've worked in Neonatal for a long time, so we get a sense of what's what.' Katie's mouth curved. 'You'll get used to it.'

'I hope so.' Phoebe gathered in a deep breath and gave her attention back to the baby. 'Right you are, little man. Let's see if we can get this over with as quickly and easily as possible. Best to do it now while you're peaceful and your mum has gone to get herself something to eat.' She looked back at Katie. 'We'll start with a blood test for bilirubin levels, and then I'll order up an abdominal X-ray. He's very jaundiced, and, given how poorly he is, and the fact that he's already three weeks old, I suspect there's more going on here than we initially thought.'

'I think you're right.' Katie nodded. 'He's not making any weight gain and his skin colour is becoming darker despite the treatments he's had so far.'

Phoebe gingerly picked up the infant, cradling the soft bundle in her arms for a minute or two and gazing down at him. 'Okay, little fellow,' she said, after a while, 'let's get this over with, shall we?'

It was around half an hour later by the time she had finished doing all the tests and returned the baby to his crib. His mother was waiting for him, and Phoebe watched as she sat down beside his cot and lightly stroked his cheek.

'I took him away to do a few tests to see what's what, but he looks comfortable enough for now, and he's none the worse for wear,' Phoebe told her, and the mother nodded, before turning her attention back to the child.

'Thanks. He looks so ill, doesn't he? Is it something I've done that's made him this way? Is it my fault?' The woman didn't look at her but there was a tremor in her voice that hinted at the strain she was under.

'No, it's nothing that you've done,' Phoebe hastened to assure her. 'You had no control over what's happening to him, I'm sure of that. His liver isn't functioning properly, but we're doing everything we can to help him through this, and I want you to know that we're here for you whenever you need us. As soon as I have all the test results I'll come back and talk to you. Don't be afraid to ask anything at all. We'll do our best to answer your questions.'

The woman seemed to be satisfied with that for the moment. 'Thank you,' she said.

Phoebe left her with the baby and went to pick up the samples she had taken, making sure that the vials were labelled and packaged correctly.

'I'm going over to the lab with these,' she told Katie. 'It'll be quicker if I take them myself. Bleep me if you need me at all.'

She left the samples and forms with the lab technician a short time later, and she was heading back towards Reception when she saw that Connor was walking in her direction. Steeling herself, she continued towards the lift bay.

His stride was long, confident and supple, and she tried not to notice how he managed to look so much like a doctor at ease with himself and the world. Why was it that everything fell into place for him as though he had been born to the job? What had happened to that rebellious young man who'd challenged the adults around him at every opportunity and had generally made his presence felt?

'Hi, there,' he said cheerfully. 'I've been wondering if I would run into you at all today. I heard that you'd been sent over to Neonatal. How's it going?' He looked at her closely. 'Not so well, from the looks of things.'

'You're right,' she answered. 'I'm not at all sure that I'm cut out for it. The babies are all so frail and ill, as though they're just clinging on to life, and I feel as though they need someone much more capable than me to take care of them.'

'You wanted more time to get used to the idea?'

She nodded. 'It was a bit of a shock to find myself posted there. Apparently I'm also supposed to attend A and E if there's a case that needs to be transferred to Neonatal. These next few months are going to be sheer hell.'

'I'm sure you'll survive.' His grey eyes met hers. 'You can always come and cry on my shoulder. I'll be here to pick up the pieces, any time.'

She gave a brief, tight smile. 'Yeah, sure you will.'

He draped an arm around her shoulders. 'You're a good doctor, Phoebe—I've heard people say as much. You qualified the year before last, didn't you, and you have the world at your fingertips. What you need is to have more confidence in yourself.'

'That's easier said than done, isn't it? It's all very well for you, in your third year after qualifying—you must already know that you've made the grade.'

She tried to keep a level tone, but it was hard for her to even think straight with his hand curved around her shoulder that way. His closeness was compelling, as though he would shield her from all life's hardships. She could feel the warmth of his fingers seeping through the cotton of her blouse, right through to her flesh, and little eddies of sensation were rippling out in ever-widening circles along her arm and the back of her neck. It was comforting and disturbing, all at the same time.

It was distracting. She shouldn't be feeling like this... She had no idea why Connor's touch should make her feel so strange. Alex was the man she cared about, the one who made her feel warm and protected, the one who made her light up inside with his smile.

Connor was the one who brought a ripple of

nervous excitement to her stomach, who filled her mind and her stomach with fluttery feelings of peculiar expectation. As a youth he had always been wayward and rebellious, a boy who had made her feel unsettled and somehow represented a sensual threat to her well-being, but as a man he was doubly so, for reasons she couldn't begin to explain to herself. All she knew was that he was to be avoided at all costs. It wouldn't do to let him pierce her defences.

'You'll do it, too. There's no doubt in my mind that you'll make the grade. You'll see, you'll work out what it is that you really want, and you'll end up with the career that satisfies you beyond all else.' He smiled down at her, his grey-blue eyes searching her face and seeking out everything she would have kept hidden from him. 'You were always the sensible one, the girl who had her priorities all worked out. People know they can rely on you, Phoebe, and that will go for the children in your care, too.'

'I'm glad you think so. I just wish I wasn't filled with so many doubts.'

'You shouldn't let them get to you. You haven't changed a bit, from what I've seen. You're cool under pressure, caring, practical and completely organised… all the things that make for a doctor who can be relied on. And you're beautiful, with it…even more beautiful than I remember.' His gaze intensified, lit by a warm glint of appreciation. 'When I saw you last night, wearing that dress that looked as though it had been sprayed on, I thought, Wow, that girl is a stunner.'

A quick flush of colour ran along her cheekbones. 'Well, thanks for that, I think…' She sent him a quizzical look. 'Not that I recall you ever commenting as such in the past. Then again, you were always too busy racketing around.'

'Not a bit of it. I had a very clear view of you…silky blonde hair shining like a halo of gold, and blue eyes as deep as the ocean. A soft, kissable mouth… What I wouldn't have given to explore the possibilities there… only you were always just that little bit out of reach…' He gazed down at her, a smile playing around his mouth. 'That was deliberate, wasn't it? You weren't ever going to let me that near you…at least, not close enough to make any kind of physical impact.'

Her brows lifted. 'Can you blame me? I saw too many girls wandering around with broken hearts, wondering where it was they had gone wrong.' She wagged a finger at him. 'But I knew where the answer lay. Their mistake was in thinking that you could ever be serious about any of them.'

Her mouth twisted slightly. 'I really don't see that things are any different now. You're just that bit older and more experienced at winding women around your little finger. I was never going to let myself be counted among them.'

She had always been well aware of Connor when they'd been young. Alex was keen to spend time with his cousin, and since she and Alex were good friends it followed that she would run into Connor every now and again.

They went around together in a group, from time to time, and she enjoyed the usual banter and camaraderie, but she was always careful to keep a guard on her heart where Connor was concerned.

She treated him to a high-voltage smile. 'And that still stands. You can cross me off your list of would-be conquests. I had the vaccination early and I'm immune.'

'And I'm cut to the quick to hear you say that.' He put on a wounded look. 'I don't know how you could imagine that I would play with your feelings that way. I practically grew up with you. I think the world of you.'

She laughed. 'Maybe. I'm sure plenty of people would believe you.' She fixed him with her gaze. 'So, tell me how things are going for you. On the work front, I mean. I expect you found your feet straight away in A and E.'

He gave a slight shrug, letting his hand drop away from her, and immediately she felt as though a draught of cold air had wafted over her. 'It's okay, I guess.'

He didn't seem to have any problem with changing the direction of the conversation, and that only confirmed her belief that he was all gloss and no substance.

'It's scary, some of the things these children get up to, though,' he added. 'You'd think they would have an inbuilt sense of self-preservation, but time and again you see them involved in accidents that might have been prevented. Only this morning I had to treat a six-year-old boy who fell thirty feet from a tree.'

She frowned. 'Is he going to be okay?'

'I think so. With any luck, there'll be no lasting damage. He has a couple of limbs in plaster, and we're keeping him under observation for a head injury, but he's better than we might have expected.'

'That's a relief.' She sighed. 'It's always boys, isn't it? It seems as though they simply have to push things to the limit when it comes to exploration and inquisitiveness.'

She wrinkled her nose at him. 'Like you, when

you filched your father's canoe and went out on the river—do you remember? That stretch of water was hazardous, and you weren't a particularly strong swimmer at the time.'

'How was I to know that I needed to be?' His expression was one of bewilderment. 'I thought the water was about two feet deep. It was only when they brought in a clean-up team a few months later that I learned the river was some eight or nine feet deep.'

She shuddered at the memory. 'No wonder my parents told me to keep away from you. You were a liability, to yourself and others.'

He laughed. 'Maybe, but it was exciting, wasn't it?'

'For you, perhaps.' To this day, she remembered the anxiety in the pit of her stomach as she'd watched him tip over into the frothing waters of the weir and come up seconds later, thrashing about and gasping for air. It had only been because he'd managed to grab hold of the canoe and cling on until it washed up against the riverbank that he was here to tell the tale. And yet it hadn't served to daunt him, had it? Just weeks later he'd been wading out further downstream, trying to catch fish with his bare hands.

'You never did learn a lesson from that, did you?' she said. 'You were back there the next day, bold as brass, showing off to all the youngsters from the village.'

'You were there, too, weren't you? I remember waving to you and you shook your head and turned your back on me.' He frowned. 'I was devastated.'

'No, you weren't. I heard you laughing and fooling about with your friends. You acted like you were the king of the river.'

He chuckled. 'Maybe. I was an idiot. I craved excitement. I wanted to prove that I could do anything I wanted. Even knowing that I was going to get it in the neck from my father didn't stop me from testing the boundaries.' He walked with her over to the lifts.

Phoebe pressed the button on the wall panel.

'I used to wonder how your poor mother coped. You have a sister, too, don't you, but at least she was never in any kind of trouble. She had far more sense than to follow in your footsteps.'

'Olivia was always going to turn out all right. She set her sights on family and children and that's exactly what she has now. She's a home-maker. It suits her to let the world pass her by.'

'But that wouldn't do for you, would it?' She studied him briefly as she heard the lift start to make its descent towards the ground floor. 'You were always a restless spirit, forever on the move. I wasn't the least bit surprised when you headed off for London. It was only later, when I heard that you had decided to go to medical school, that you did something unexpected with your life.'

His glance trailed over her. 'You have no faith in me at all, do you? I can see that we have a lot of catching up to do.' He smiled. 'Are you free for lunch today? It might be pleasant to take a walk in the woodland close by here. It starts just at the back of the hospital, and we could enjoy the spring sunshine for a while.'

She shook her head. 'I'm afraid I'm not. I said I would meet up with Alex in the cafeteria at lunchtime, but you'd be welcome to join us if you wanted. My break starts at 1.30. Alex isn't having too great a time, by all accounts, and I want to give him some moral support. Jessica saw him earlier and said he was a bit down in the mouth.'

Connor made a wry face. 'That's a shame—for Alex, and for us. It would have been good to have the chance to talk for longer, just you and me.' He tilted his head a little to one side. 'You're very fond of Alex still, aren't you? I wasn't really surprised to find that you two are living together.'

Her mouth flattened. 'We're not living together, as you so bluntly put it. We just happen to share the same house. Jessica lives there, too, remember?'

'I do. But you and Alex go way back, don't you? I still catch you looking at him with those moon eyes, as though he's sugar candy wrapped up in exotic packaging.'

She laughed. 'Jealous, are you? Poor Connor. That must be a very odd experience for you.' She lightly patted his hand. 'You'll get over it, I'm sure. You were never one to worry over lost opportunities. There's always another one just around the corner.'

'You're a cruel woman, and you have me all wrong, you know.' He made a good attempt at a crestfallen face, but Phoebe was wise to his antics.

The lift doors swished open. 'I have to go,' she said, stepping inside. 'There are several babies who need me much more than you do. Perhaps I'll see you later, back at the house.'

He nodded and waved a hand in acknowledgement as the lift doors closed on her, and once the lift started to move and he was out of her field of vision she relaxed a little, letting out a long, slow sigh and allowing her shoulders to slump a fraction. Somehow, she hadn't realised how much the tension had been building up inside her as she had spoken to Connor, or how much she had relied on her senses to help her to stay on alert. He was a threat to her in every way imaginable, and it was sheer relief to be moving out of range.

Alex, on the other hand, was a much easier person to get along with. There were no worries with him. She knew what to expect, and he was always there for her, just as she was there for him.

'Is the consultant giving you a hard time?' she asked Alex as they collected their lunch trays in the hospital restaurant a couple of hours later. 'I was hoping that things would be going smoothly for you.'

'He's watching me like a hawk. I think he remembers me from a year or so back. He thinks I have promise, but need a push to live up to it.'

'So he's going in hard, right from the beginning? It seems a bit strange to be doing that this early on.'

His mouth twisted. 'I was supposed to have done some groundwork on a few of the case notes before starting ward rounds with him today. Usually I wouldn't have had too many problems with that, but someone dropped the files and it was all a bit of a scramble to put things together again in time. I had to think on my feet and hope that everything would be all right. I don't think the consultant was too impressed.'

Phoebe carried her tray to a table by the window. 'I can't help thinking that it's a bit unfair really, to come down so hard on you right from the outset, but I'm sure you'll manage to sort things out. You've a good, clear head on your shoulders, and you're brilliant with the patients. Your boss is bound to see that, given time.'

He grimaced. 'I hope so. I suppose he's only doing his job, keeping me on my toes. I started off on the wrong foot, wanting to do A and E instead, but things don't always go according to plan...like you with the neonatal. I wish we could have been working together, Phoebe. I always seem to get along so much better when you're around. It's as though everything magically falls into place around you.'

She chuckled at that, and started to eat her lunch, twirling spaghetti around her fork with a deft hand. 'If only… I could do with a magic touch, up on Neonatal.'

Alex ate a mouthful of steak pie. 'I think Connor was there when they handed out the pixie dust,' he said after a moment or two. 'Everything he touches seems to go his way. Did you see the car he's driving around in?'

Phoebe shook her head. 'I came in with Jessica this morning. We set out some fifteen minutes after Connor left, and I guessed he must have parked in the garage block last night.' She flicked a glance at him. 'Is it something special?'

'A midnight-blue convertible. I can't believe he landed on his feet so well… I know his family have money, but he always reckoned he'd make his own way in the world.'

'Perhaps he changed his mind.'

'Yeah, maybe.' Alex finished off his food and glanced across the room. 'Talk of the devil.'

Phoebe blinked. 'He's here?'

Alex nodded. Her glance followed his, and met with Connor's piercing gaze.

'Pity he left it so late to put in an appearance, or we might have had a chat.' Alex glanced at the watch on his wrist. 'I have to be getting back to Orthopaedics. I want to get on the good side of my boss, and if I show him I can put in extra time, it might help things along.'

He pushed his chair back and stood up, coming around the table to give Phoebe a swift embrace. 'It was good being able to have lunch together,' he said. 'You've helped me to put a bright face on things.'

She smiled up at him. 'You'll be fine,' she murmured. She laid a hand lightly on his arm. 'Just remember what it was that made you decide to become a doctor in the first place. You were so good at helping people when you volunteered with the rescue services that they all thought it was something you should follow up on. That still stands, to this day.'

He brushed the back of his hand gently over her cheek. 'And you're a treasure. Remind me to pay you back some day.'

Phoebe flashed him a mischievous grin. 'You can do that by remembering to get the groceries in. If you don't, you'll have Jessica to reckon with.'

'Oh, no. Save me from that.' Alex started to walk away from the table, raising a hand in greeting to Connor as he went.

Phoebe looked across the room at Connor. He wasn't alone. He was with a senior house officer from A and E, a pretty girl who Phoebe had chatted with from time to time. The woman's cheeks were faintly flushed, and Phoebe guessed she was finding it all too easy to fall for Connor's charm.

Phoebe's mouth took on a wry slant. It hadn't taken him long to find someone willing to take her place by his side this lunchtime, had it? Were the two of them coming in here to grab a sandwich after a pleasant stroll along the leafy paths that threaded through the woods nearby? Why did that thought needle her so much?

It was the supreme confidence of the man… that must be it. As Alex had said, Connor managed to land on his feet every time.

CHAPTER THREE

'YOU'RE very quiet. Is everything all right?' Phoebe glanced at Jessica as they tended to the flowerbeds in the garden at the back of the house. She pulled up a handful of chickweed and tossed it into a bucket.

'It's fine.' Jessica stood up and placed her hands on the back of her hips, stretching her spine as though she was aching a little.

'You don't have to do this with me, you know.' Phoebe shielded her eyes from the sun as she looked up at her friend. 'I like being out here, and I find that I can think things through more easily if I spend some time tidying up the garden, but I know it's not everyone's cup of tea.'

'It isn't that…I think plants brighten the place

up, and this is such a small area that it doesn't take much to look after it. It's more of a courtyard, really, isn't it, but it's great to sit out here and enjoy the lovely summer weather.' Jessica flopped down into a wrought-iron chair by the round table and helped herself to a glass of fruit juice. 'Shall I pour one for you?' She lifted the glass jug and raised a brow in query.

'Yes, please. I'm parched.' Phoebe pulled off her cotton gardening gloves and went to sit down opposite her.

She took a moment to look around. The walls of the house were white-painted, reflecting the warmth of the sun, so that it was pleasant to sit out here and while away an hour or so. At intervals, the walls were covered with rectangles of wooden trellis, where jasmine scrambled and filled the air with delicate perfume. Stone planters were placed at strategic points on the terrace, filled with bright pansies, adding colour here and there.

Phoebe looked again at her friend. She was

faintly concerned. Despite Jessica's light-hearted chatter, she couldn't help thinking that something was bothering her, and the garden talk was a cover-up. 'How are things going with Mr Kirk and his team? Is it all turning out as you hoped it might?'

Jessica pulled a face. 'Not exactly.' She might have said more, but Connor emerged from the house just then and came to join them.

'So there you are. I wondered where you had all gone. I just came back from the garage and the house was empty.' He looked from one to the other. 'You've a smudge on your face, Phoebe… leaf green. It's quite fetching, but it doesn't quite go with the peaches-and-cream look. Want me to rub it off for you?'

He moved towards her, his hands at the ready, and Phoebe inched herself back in her seat, avoiding his seeking fingers. 'I'll do it myself, thanks.' It was a plague on her nervous system that he was here at all, without him attempting to lay his hands on her. She pulled a tissue from her pocket and rubbed vigorously at her cheek.

His mouth curved, and he turned his attention to Jessica. 'What's up, Jess? You don't look too happy. It's because you'd rather be down the pub, isn't it?'

Jessica threw an ice cube at him. 'At this time of day? Are you mad?' She wrinkled her nose. 'Well, yes, actually…maybe I would.' She let out a short laugh. 'But it wouldn't do when I'm supposed to go on duty in a couple of hours. Late shift…ugh.'

'Same here.' Connor frowned. 'So what's with Mr Kirk and his team? I heard what you were saying just now. Is he giving you a hard time?'

'Not really.' Jessica was thoughtful for a moment. 'It's just that there's something about his manner that bothers me a bit. I do my best, but he can be a bit aloof sometimes. It's hard to know what he's thinking because he has this way of keeping his distance… He's like it with the patients, too. A sort of I-know-best, paternal kind of attitude that really ought to have died out long ago. Still, he's rated very highly. I've heard he's a top-rate surgeon and he's known for getting results and working on new procedures. I expect I'll learn a lot from him.'

Connor put his feet up on one of the empty chairs, crossing his legs at the ankles. 'You shouldn't let him get to you. It doesn't do for doctors to get above themselves. These days they're open to scrutiny.' The fabric of his trousers pulled tautly across his thighs and Phoebe averted her gaze.

She still didn't know why he was actually living here with them. His parents had a big house that wasn't too far away from here, and surely it would have been better for him to stay with them?

She said softly, 'I expect Mr Kirk knows that, but doesn't much care.' She sent Connor a quick glance. 'He's very confident in his abilities—in fact, in some respects he reminds me of you. You never seem to falter or question what you do. It appears to me that you look over a situation, decide what to do about it and move on...like choosing to come here when you had opportunities waiting for you in London. Better ones than you were offered here, according to Alex.'

His gaze narrowed on her. Did he suspect that she was wishing he were elsewhere? If he did, he made no comment. Instead, he answered cautiously, 'It's all a bit subjective, isn't it? I could have stayed to do a six-month stint in trauma surgery, but this rotation in A and E was more tempting. Besides, I thought it would be pleasant to spend the spring and summer months by the sea in my home county.'

'I suppose I can see the logic in that.' She reached for the jug and poured out more juice, adding ice from an insulated pot. 'What do your parents think about you coming back here to Devon? They must be pleased to have you on their doorstep once more.'

He nodded. 'My mother was glad to have me close by. My father is busy with the business as usual, but even he manages to take a break at the weekends, so it's all worked out fairly well.'

'You didn't ever think of going to live at

home? I would have thought that would be the cheaper option.'

His mouth tilted, and she knew then that he had picked up on her train of thought. 'Maybe,' he said, a glitter of amusement starting up in his eyes, 'but, as I said, I was quite taken with the option of living by the coast, and since Alex and I are related to one another it seemed like a good option to stay here. My parents' house is further inland…just like your family home. Did you not think of going to stay there?'

She leaned back in her chair. 'It crossed my mind, but I wanted to be independent. Besides, my sister and her children often stay over at the house, and it would have been a bit of a squeeze if I'd been living there, too. My parents only have a three-bedroomed place, unlike your country mansion.'

He blinked, sending her a wry smile. 'I wouldn't exactly call it that. It's bigger than average, I guess, but mansion? Never.'

'Anyway,' Phoebe murmured, 'our old house

doesn't come anywhere near what you enjoyed, but my mother loves it when the family are around. She likes to fuss over her grandchildren, especially with little Emily being so poorly as a baby. The children bring out all her maternal instincts.' She swallowed her ice-cold drink. 'It suits me to visit on a regular basis.'

'I can imagine. I remember what a lovely atmosphere there was when I first used to visit,' Connor said, nodding. 'Your parents made a wonderful, welcoming home and I could see how happy you were as a family…on the instances when I was allowed to call in and see you, that is. Things changed after I grew older. I became the wild boy from over the hill, and they had me down as a bad influence, didn't they?' He made a rueful grimace. 'I can't say that I blame them.'

Phoebe stared down at the liquid in her glass. She had been resentful of the ban at first. For all he had landed in trouble on a regular basis, Connor had always managed to tug at her heartstrings. Maybe that was why she had gone looking for him that day when he'd gone missing at the end of her fifteenth summer. It had been as though there was an almost telepathic bond between them, and she had sensed that something was seriously wrong.

Jessica's face lit up with curiosity. 'You were wild? Oh, I can just imagine it. You still have that look about you as though the devil's lurking in there somewhere.' She grinned impishly. 'I'm intrigued. Tell me more.'

'Nope. Will not.' Connor sent her a teasing glance. 'I shall keep my murky past to myself, and leave you in suspense. All I will say is that Phoebe's parents were probably right to warn her off me, and Phoebe showed a lot more common sense than you might have expected for a girl of her tender years. She always followed her instincts, and I expect that's why she and Alex bond together so well. He's protective of her, and in return she gives him the stability he needs.'

'Alex—huh…he's a liability.' Jessica's tone was scornful. 'What he needs is a good shaking.'

'See—we all have our faults.' Connor yawned and then stretched, as though preparing for action, his movements supple like a tiger's, and Phoebe watched, unwillingly drawn to follow the way his long body uncoiled.

'I have to get ready for work,' he said. 'Does anyone want a lift in to the hospital?'

'Oh, yes, please.' Jessica straightened, preparing to stand up. 'I've been waiting for you to ask. How could anyone resist a spin in that beautiful car?'

He smiled, and glanced at Phoebe. 'And you? We all finish work around the same time, don't we?'

She shook her head. 'I'll stick with my runabout, thanks. That way I can come and go as I please.'

'Independent to the last,' he murmured. 'One day, Phoebe, one day…'

She had no idea what he meant by that. 'Yes, one day I'll find out what it is I truly want,' she said, 'and then the world will be my oyster.'

Things certainly weren't going the way she wanted right now. At work, she struggled every day to come to terms with working with vulnerable babies, and it was no different when she arrived at the hospital a short time later. In fact, it looked as though things were about to get worse.

'They're calling for you over in A and E,' Katie told her as soon as she walked into the neonatology unit.

Phoebe frowned. 'What's the problem, do you know?'

'A traffic accident, as far as I understand it. A woman gave birth prematurely as a result, and it looks as though the baby is in difficulty. The parents are both injured and being treated right now. I think A and E want you to go and help with the baby and bring her over to Neonatology.'

Phoebe sucked in a quick breath. 'Okay, tell them I'm on my way.'

Things were not going well when she arrived in the A and E department. The parents had been whisked off to the operating theatre, and the paediatric team working with the baby was concerned about the infant's frail condition.

'She's not breathing,' the nurse said, her expression anxious. 'I've applied suction, but she's still not responding.'

Phoebe helped to resuscitate the infant. 'Her heart rate is very slow,' she said. Already she was reaching for the bag and mask oxygen equipment. After trying to inflate the baby's lungs for a short time, she shook her head. 'There's little chest movement.' There was a note of urgency in her voice. 'I'm going to have to put in a tube to help her to breathe. We need to get her on a ventilator as soon as possible.'

It was some half an hour later, after she had linked the infant to a heart monitor and taped a cannula in place at a vein in her arm so that they could administer medication, that she was ready to take her over to the neonatal unit.

'Poor little scrap,' the nurse said. 'What a way to come into the world.'

Phoebe nodded. It was scary to think that her mother and father were both undergoing operations in attempts to save their lives. 'Let's hope the parents make a good recovery. As to this little one, her lungs are still immature, and she needs all the help we can give her.'

She glanced into the next treatment bay as she prepared to set off for the lift that would take her up to Neonatal. Connor was there, attending to a young boy of around eight years old, and for a moment she paused, drawn to watch him in action.

The child was distressed and struggling to breathe, and she guessed that he was suffering from a worrying asthma attack. It looked as though he was in a bad state, but Connor was talking quietly to him all the time, his manner gentle and soothing.

'This will help you, Charlie,' he was saying. 'Just relax and try to breathe in and let the medication seep into your lungs. It will help to open up your air passages and make you feel better.' His voice was calm and evenly modulated, falling softly on Phoebe's ears, and she realised that there was an almost hypnotic quality about it.

The boy nodded, and Connor glanced down at his football shirt. 'It looks as though you support the same team that I do,' he said. 'They did all right at their last match, didn't they? Except for Bex having two left feet and falling over his boots. I don't know where his head was that day, but it wasn't with him on the pitch, was it?'

The boy chuckled, and Connor went on, 'Mind you, he made up for it with the penalty shot. Talk about whacking it in. It hit the back of the net so hard I thought the goalposts were going to tip over.'

Charlie appeared to relax. His breathing was much easier now, and Phoebe could see that he was almost out of danger. Clearly, Charlie was in good hands.

Connor turned and glanced towards her as she started on her way once more. She nodded to him and he gave her the thumbs-up sign.

'Hi, there, Phoebe,' he said cheerfully. 'How

about supper in the hospital restaurant later on, since you stood me up the other day? Jessica said she'd try to drop by around seven o'clock, and Alex is hoping he'll be free by then.'

'That sounds okay,' she agreed. It would be good to catch up with Alex and find out if he was coping with Orthopaedics any better. Lately, with their different shift patterns, they had been like ships that passed in the night. 'I'll see if I can get away.' She glanced at the baby in the incubator. There were no signs of respiratory distress, but her heart rate was still slow, and her oxygen saturation could have been better. 'I have to go,' she said. 'This baby's had a hard time coming into the world, and I need to get her up to the unit as quickly as possible.'

'I heard about that,' he murmured. 'I'll see you later.'

As she moved away, she heard him say to the boy, 'Now, there goes one very pretty doctor, don't you think? She almost makes me wish I was ill so that she could come and pat my brow with a damp cloth.'

The boy giggled.

Phoebe went on her way. The man was incorrigible, but he certainly had a magic touch where the boy was concerned.

She was more than ready for her break when suppertime came around. The baby had been suffering from seizures, and they were all worried for her safety.

'You go off and get something to eat,' Katie told her. 'You've been on duty for hours, and it will do nobody any good if you start to wilt. It's quiet enough around here for the moment.'

Phoebe acknowledged the truth of that, and made her way down to the restaurant on the ground floor. Connor was already in there. He looked as fresh and energetic as if he had only just come on duty, and it was all she could do not to scowl at him. 'I don't know how you manage it,' she said. 'How do you stay so jaunty and unruffled? It's as though nothing touches you.'

'It comes from years of practice.' He nodded towards the glass doors at the side of the restaurant. 'Shall we go and sit out there? There aren't too many people in the courtyard just now. It will be peaceful.'

'Okay. I'll come and join you just as soon as I've collected my food.' There was no sign of Jessica or Alex, and it was already after seven o'clock. Perhaps they wouldn't be able to make it down.

She chose a light cheese salad with crusty bread and a fruit tart to follow. Connor cast a swift glance over her tray as she set it down on the table. 'It's no wonder that you never put on any weight,' he said. 'You don't eat enough to keep a sparrow alive.'

She gave him a withering smile. 'Unlike you. I don't know where you put it all—and yet you never add an ounce of fat to your waistline, do you? You're all lean and fit, as though you've just come from working out in the gym.' Her eyes narrowed. 'In fact, I suspect that's what you do. Otherwise, it's just not fair.'

He laughed, and stabbed his fork into a substantial cottage pie. His gaze wandered over her, taking in the fullness of her curves beneath the light cotton top she was wearing, and then drifted down over her narrow-fitting skirt to explore the length of her shapely legs. 'It has to be said, though you'd still look good even with extra padding.'

Her cheeks heated under that appreciative scrutiny. To distract herself from the hectic play of emotions that he evoked in her, she fixed him with an exasperated stare. 'That's it, isn't it? That's what you do all the time…you lead people astray. It's what you did when you encouraged your friends to stay out all night on Exmoor, and it's what you did when you produced those bottles of cider a few weeks after you turned sixteen. You shared them among your friends. No thought for the consequences, just live for the moment.' She glowered at him. 'Just try telling Jessica to pile on the pounds, and she'll give you short shrift.'

He paused, his fork midway between his plate and his mouth. 'Now, there you have one lady I wouldn't like to cross.' He nodded, a brooding expression on his face. 'When she gets that look in her eyes, I know she means business.'

Phoebe took a sip of her coffee. 'I doubt a little bit of trouble would bother you. I heard that you were still causing mayhem, even here in the hospital.'

His brows lifted. 'You must have me confused with someone else. What kind of mayhem would I be causing?'

'There was a rumour going round about you trying to change how things were organised around here—something about improving waiting times and persuading doctors to treat more patients.' She frowned. 'It seems to me that you're quite likely to be treading on toes with that kind of venture. Didn't you have a word with Mr Kirk about the waiting list for some of the cardiology patients?'

His eyes widened. 'Word certainly gets around in this place, doesn't it? Why should it matter if I decide to have a chat with a few people?'

'You know very well why. The consultants

won't like it if you start making waves. You're still a junior doctor as far as they're concerned. Besides, you don't even work in cardiology.'

He shrugged, and speared broccoli with his fork. 'I don't see the point in keeping quiet when I know that things can be put right. We have theatres that aren't in use at the weekend. How many more patients could be treated all the sooner if we made proper use of the facilities?'

She made a wry smile. 'So, if you became a consultant, you'd be prepared to give up your weekends and spend them working in Theatre or seeing patients, would you?'

'Of course. It goes without saying. You bring in a rota system and keep things moving. There's too much inertia holding people back. What we need is to bring about change and shake things up.'

'Hmm. You won't last long in the medical profession if you go about rattling cages like that. There are some powerful people running the hospitals, and they won't thank you for stirring things up.' She sent him a thoughtful glance.

'Perhaps you should wait until you're a fully fledged consultant yourself before you start getting up people's noses.'

'Nah. That would be totally boring, and I doubt I could wait that long.' He pushed his empty plate to one side and reached for his apple pie. 'I leave it to people like you, Missy Play Safe, to follow the rules and support the status quo.'

She pretended to be affronted. 'Well, thanks a lot for that. If you're going to be insulting I'll have to think twice about joining you for supper another time.' She frowned. 'And don't think I haven't sussed out that I'm here under false pretences. Jessica and Alex aren't going to put in an appearance, are they?'

'Ah…' A momentary flush of guilt washed over his face. 'I meant to tell you about that. Jess has been asked to help out in Theatre with a cardiac case—the man who was involved in the accident earlier today—and Alex is looking after the woman who gave birth to the little girl who's up in Neonatal. She suffered a leg injury, among other things, in the crash, and they're keeping her under observation.'

She gave a heavy sigh. 'It's a tragedy, isn't it? Three lives devastated.'

'It is…but with any luck they'll come through this in one piece, eventually.'

'I hope so.' She winced. 'The baby isn't doing so well. She needs specialist help, and the consultant is thinking of transferring her to the children's hospital in Somerset.'

He nodded. 'Yes, I heard that. I spoke to my boss about it, and it looks as though they'll be assembling a neonatal transport team to take her over there. It's possible I'll be part of it. My rotation is supposed to cover the full spectrum of paediatric A and E so that would be another one to notch up for my specialist training.'

She looked at him and blinked, trying to take that in. Her name was already down to be part of that team…which could only mean that they would be travelling together. That was not good news.

She kept her feelings to herself. 'Alex would have given anything to be able to do that.'

Connor's glance trailed over her. 'Yes, well, I'm sorry that I took his job from him. It wasn't personal. I know you wanted to work with him, but I'm afraid it looks as though you're going to be stuck with me. Our paths are likely to cross on a regular basis, given the nature of the rotation.'

He discarded his spoon in his now empty dessert bowl. 'Perhaps I could make up for whatever it is I've done wrong, or may do wrong at some time in the future, by taking you out somewhere special. It'll be late when we finish here tonight, but we could go and try out the new Blue Bay Club, if you like. It's open till the small hours, and neither of us has to work until tomorrow afternoon, do we?'

She shook her head. 'Thanks for the offer, but I don't think I'll take you up on it this time,' she murmured. 'Alex asked if I would drive him home later. His car is being serviced, and we were planning on stopping off at the Griddle Bar for half an hour or so after work.'

Connor's mouth twisted. 'I thought it strange that you weren't too worried about him not putting in an appearance. I always seem to come in too late, don't I? How about if I book a date with you for tomorrow and maybe another one for the day after that?' He spooned sugar into his cup and began to stir the coffee. 'I suppose you've already made arrangements for then, too, haven't you?'

She gave him a thoughtful glance. 'As it happens, I have, but that shouldn't come as too much of a surprise to you, should it? After all, you were the one who called me Missy Play Safe. Perhaps you ought to familiarise yourself with my other title, Missy All Planned Out. That way, you'll always know what to expect, won't you?'

His mouth took on a rueful expression as he watched her over his coffee-cup, and Phoebe smiled as she tasted her fruit tart. Was he finally getting the message?

Somehow, it was a bitter-sweet victory.

CHAPTER FOUR

'So, is your car running smoothly now?' Phoebe met up with Alex as they both headed for the doctors' lounge. 'Has the garage mechanic managed to sort everything out for you?'

'Yes, he has, and it's good,' he said, nodding and pushing open the door for her. 'Not that it will ever match up to Connor's speed fiend.' His eyes narrowed and he looked thoroughly put out. 'I didn't think I'd ever be green with envy, but if you were to colour me all over in grass, spinach and lime jelly with emerald sprinkles, then you have it. I don't think I'll ever be the same again.'

She laughed. 'Poor Alex. What are we going to do with you? Nothing ever goes quite the way it should, does it?' She went over to the worktop at the side of the room and lifted up the coffee-pot. 'Tell me you're getting on better in Orthopaedics, at least.'

'It isn't too bad, I suppose.' He came to stand beside her and pulled two mugs down from a shelf. 'I've been putting in extra hours on the job to cover for people on sick leave, and that seems to have gone down fairly well with my boss. I'm just a bit worried because I've been pulled out of the training day seminars on a couple of occasions to attend emergencies, and that's not going to bode well for my monthly review meeting.'

Connor must have come into the room while they were pouring coffee, because he appeared alongside them and said, 'Training days are supposed to be protected. You should talk to your consultant about that.'

'Oh, sure, and he's going to have me down as a complainer, isn't he? Where will that leave me when the references are being written?'

Connor shrugged and helped himself to coffee. 'Sometimes you have to make a stand, and stick up for what's right.'

'Yeah, right. Coming from someone who can always fall back on Daddy's money to keep him going if the worst comes to the worst, I'd say that was rich—if you'll forgive the pun.'

'I've no idea what you're talking about,' Connor murmured. 'I don't rely on my father for anything, least of all his money. What I have is mine through my own endeavours.'

'Did I get it all wrong?' Disgruntled, Alex took his coffee over to the window and gazed out briefly at the landscaped gardens, before turning around once more. 'Sorry…but you seem to have done pretty well for yourself, all the same. And you always land on your feet, don't you?' Alex's eyes took on a mischievous glint. 'I couldn't help noticing that the new senior house officer in children's A and E—Lisa, is it?—was bowled over with your flash car. I heard you had taken her out in it.'

'She needed a lift home.' Connor's gaze was thoughtful. 'Is that a problem for you?'

Alex's mouth turned down at the corners. 'Take no notice of me. It's pure sour grapes. I'm just jealous because I don't have a sleek roadster for myself. It's my own fault. I should have worked harder…or invested in oil when the price was right.'

He drank his coffee and threw Connor a mischievous glance. 'Things worked out all right for you with Lisa, though, didn't they? I heard you and she were all cosied up in her new house last night. Nice one.'

'You don't miss much, do you?' Connor fixed him with a steady gaze. 'Or is this the hospital grapevine working at full speed?'

Alex chuckled. 'You know how it is. The nurses work with the senior house officers, and there's a bit of gossip here and a long chat there… Before you know it, all your secrets are aired.'

'Then maybe it's fortunate I don't have any secrets to be made public,' Connor murmured.

He swallowed his coffee and glanced at Phoebe. 'Are we on for the neonatal transport this afternoon? Katie told me they were hoping the baby would be in a stable enough condition to undertake the move.'

She nodded. 'Her vital signs are not too bad at the moment, so it looks as though it will go ahead.'

Despite the coffee there was a hollow feeling in the pit of her stomach. She had been wondering why Connor hadn't returned home last night. He hadn't been there when she'd come back to the house from the Griddle Bar around midnight, and there had been no sign of his car returning in the early hours. That morning, as Jessica had pointed out to her, his room had been empty and the bed hadn't been slept in.

She glanced at him. Wasn't that the same shirt he had been wearing yesterday? Her mouth flattened. It hadn't taken him long to find a new object for his affections, had it? Had Lisa been wined and dined at the Blue Bay? Somehow, it rankled that he had been able to replace her so easily.

For the life of her, she didn't know why him staying out all night bothered her so much, but perhaps it would serve as a timely warning to her to keep her distance. He was fickle, and his affections could be diverted as easily as thistle-down blowing on the wind.

She rinsed her coffee-cup under the tap and headed for the door. 'I have to go and check on a new arrival in A and E,' she said. 'I'll catch up with you later, Alex.'

Alex nodded. 'Maybe we could get together some time this week? Perhaps Thursday evening, if you're not going to be working?'

'That sounds fine to me.' She went out of the door and walked along the corridor to the stairs. It gave her a breathing space, a chance to get herself together, but Connor caught up with her as she reached the flight to the ground floor.

'Not taking the lift today?' he commented. 'I hope this has nothing to do with diets and losing weight. You look perfect to me, just as you are.' His gaze shifted over her, taking in the soft lines of her blouse and the gentle drape of her skirt as it flowed around her legs.

'Thanks. I'm aiming to stay that way. You can call this aerobic exercise, if you like.'

He made a smile. 'If you say so.' His expression sobered. 'You didn't look too happy, back there in the doctors' lounge. Is everything okay?'

'Of course.' Not for one moment would she dream of telling him what had really been on her mind. But, then, she hadn't been too keen to get back to work, had she, in her heart of hearts? 'I suppose, if the truth be known, I'm worrying about the baby who was brought to A and E this morning. I can't seem to get used to dealing with these fragile little infants. The very first baby I treated today needed an operation to correct a blockage in the flow of bile from the liver to the gallbladder. He wasn't very well at all.'

Connor was thoughtful. 'I've heard that there's more chance of a reasonable recovery if the operation is carried out in the early weeks—is it likely that things will work out well for him?'

She nodded. 'The operation went well, so I'm reasonably confident that he'll be all right, but he's just one among many infants who need our attention. These babies arrive here with so many different conditions affecting them, most of them serious and all of them very worrying—like the baby that has just been admitted. He has a heart defect that's causing him to go downhill fast, by all accounts.'

Connor's expression became serious. 'Yes, I was the one who examined him earlier and arranged for him to be admitted.'

'Oh, I see. I didn't realise that.' By now they had reached the A and E unit, and she waited while Connor keyed in his code so that the doors swished open.

'The poor little scrap has a number of problems to contend with,' he said as they walked into the department. 'He isn't feeding well, his breathing is rapid and there's a bluish colour around his mouth and nose. I've done a chest X-ray and I suspect that he's developing congestive heart failure.'

Phoebe gave a shuddery sigh as she passed by the reception desk. 'It doesn't sound good at all, does it? I'll go and take a look at him and transfer him to the neonatal unit. I imagine I'll have to put in a call to Mr Kirk for him to come and do a consultation.'

'Yes, that's what I was thinking.' He sent her a quick glance. 'Is something wrong? You look very pale all of a sudden.'

'I'm all right.' She stiffened her shoulders. 'I just have to brace myself to deal with these things. It's just that I find these kinds of cases particularly hard as I first witnessed it with my sister's little girl, Emily, and since then I'm always afraid that things are not going to turn out well for children with these kinds of problems. I remember the heartache we all went through with Emily when she was a baby, and I'm not sure how I would cope if things were to go badly for any child in my care. That's why I wasn't happy about this particular rotation, even though I didn't have any real choice but to do it.'

'You hadn't done any medical training when Emily was going through all her initial problems,' he said, frowning. 'You were bound to feel apprehensive and upset. You didn't do anything wrong—you just did the best that you could at the time.'

Phoebe shook her head. 'But my best wasn't good enough. I still remember the panic I felt when my sister came to me and told me how ill the baby was. I didn't know what to do, and I felt useless. She was looking to me to help her, and I should have been able to do something.'

'As I heard it, you gave the baby chest compressions and mouth-to-mouth while you were waiting for the ambulance to arrive. I don't see that you could have done any more in the circumstances.' He came to a halt by the computer bay where doctors usually sat to write up their notes.

Phoebe glanced around distractedly. 'Maybe. I don't know. It still doesn't sit easily with me. This is my family that we're talking about. They mean the world to me and I felt as though I let them down.'

His glance travelled over her. 'You did more than could have been expected. Your sister told me all about it some time later when she brought Emily to London for a hospital consultation. She said she had been scared back then because she had no idea what to do. She was the older sister, but she turned to you because you were always so capable in a crisis.'

'All I do recall is that Emily went into convulsions in the ambulance and I couldn't do anything but look on and pray that she would survive.' Phoebe grimaced. 'I think it must have been the worst moment of my life.'

He reached for her hand and held it between his palms. 'Wasn't it also the factor that made you decide to take up medicine as a career?'

'I suppose so.' She wriggled and tried to move back a pace, but he was not about to let her go. His hold on her was gentle but firm, and as he moved closer to her she knew that somehow she had to break away from him before she became wrapped up in the nebulous, enticing security blanket he was busy weaving around her.

'Of course it was. You made up your mind that you just had to go out of your way to look after people.' He smiled into her eyes. 'That's what makes you so lovable.'

Lovable? She gazed up at him, her eyes widening. Why had he used that word out of all the ones he might have chosen? It didn't mean anything, though, did it? It was just a casual phrase, dropped into the melting pot of her confused emotions. Why was she even giving it a second thought?

She looked down at the hands that clasped hers. They were warm and protective, the long fingers lightly tanned to a golden brown, and the sense of well-being they induced travelled along her arm and invaded the whole of her body. It was because he was holding her...that was the reason she was feeling so mixed up, wasn't it? Her mind simply refused to function properly while he was doing that.

'I don't know about any of that,' she murmured. 'But I'm rapidly coming to the conclusion that I should steer clear of paediatrics throughout the rest of my training. Treating adults is one thing, but I'm beginning to realise that working with infants and children is altogether too stressful for me. I've had to watch Emily these last few years, growing up with a heart condition, needing constant care and attention, and I saw how worrying it was for my sister, bracing herself to prepare her child for different procedures.'

'But Emily is doing fine now, isn't she?' Connor lightly stroked her arm. 'All that care and attention has paid off in the end.'

'Yes, you're right, but it was hard watching her go through it.' She glanced to one side at the perspex board where patients' names were listed. 'My little charge is in bay four. I'll go and see how he's doing.'

Connor nodded. 'Drop by when you've had time to assess him and let me know what's what.

I'll be in the paediatric observation ward. I have to go and look at a couple of patients who were admitted overnight. One of them had a heart operation recently, but he collapsed last night and I have to explain to the parents about changes to his medication.'

'Okay.'

He let go of her and Phoebe hurried away before he could lure her back to his side.

Connor appeared to have no problem at all in dealing with his small patients or their parents. She'd seen evidence of it on a number of occasions when she had passed through children's A and E, and everybody said how good he was at working with them. It would be great if some of his confidence would rub off on her.

Some half an hour later, when she had finished checking over the baby and had gathered together all the paperwork that needed to go along with him to the neonatal unit, she went in search of Connor once more.

'Are you busy?' she asked him, wheeling the

baby into the treatment room where he was working. 'Only I need you to sign off on these papers before I can take the baby up to the unit.'

She smiled at the child Connor was tending, a young boy of around nine years old, who was lying in the bed, propped up by pillows. Then she nodded a greeting to the parents who were by his side.

Connor came over to her. 'Yes, of course. I'm glad that you're here.' His grey eyes took on a warm, inviting glimmer. 'You can perhaps help to explain to Mr and Mrs Brannigan about the holiday centre on Exmoor. I think you're familiar with it because that's where your little niece went to take a break a few months ago.'

Phoebe glanced at the parents. 'Are you talking about the activity centre?'

Mrs Brannigan nodded. 'That's right. I was thinking of taking Jamie there for a few days while my husband is away on business. Jamie's recovering from a heart operation, and he's been feeling quite miserable lately, so I was looking for somewhere that would be fun for him, but not too strenuous. Can you recommend it at all?'

Phoebe nodded, and looked across the room at Jamie once more. 'I think you would like it there, Jamie,' she said. 'My niece was a little younger than you when she first went to the centre. She was six years old and, like you, she had just had an operation, and she tired easily, but there were all sorts of exciting things for her to do at the activity centre. She went again last year, because she enjoyed it so much.'

She gave the boy an encouraging smile. 'There's wheelchair access, and you can do things like canoeing and fishing, or if you don't like watersports there are always things like the farm animals to see—Emily liked the horse riding while we were there, but sometimes, if she was feeling less energetic, she spent time in the craft centre. There would be children of around your age staying there, so you could perhaps make some new friends.'

Jamie looked pleased with what she told him,

and glanced towards his mother. 'I think I might like that,' he said. 'Could we do that?'

Mrs Brannigan was cautious. 'I'm still not sure, Jamie.' She turned to Connor. 'The thing is, I don't know how I would cope if he had any problems while we were there. I really want him to have some fun, but there are so many things I need to bear in mind, like sorting out the medication he needs, and what to do if he has any more after-effects from the operation…like the way he collapsed last night. We still need to learn to adjust to his condition.' She looked at her son. 'I know I said that I would take you away for a break after the operation, but perhaps it's too soon.'

Jamie looked crestfallen and appealed to his father. 'It'll be all right, won't it, Dad? Tell Mum it'll be all right. I'm getting stronger every day.'

His father looked uncomfortable. 'I don't know, Jamie. You're still quite frail. Perhaps your mother's right. We ought to wait until you've managed to put on a bit more weight, and you're feeling better. We hadn't expected any of these complications, and I won't be there to help out, will I?'

'There is another solution, perhaps,' Connor put in. 'You were planning on going there at the end of next week, weren't you?'

Mrs Brannigan nodded. 'That's right. I'd made a tentative booking, but after he collapsed I had second thoughts about it.'

Connor nodded. 'That's understandable, but I might be able to come along and help you out for a couple of days at the weekend, if that would be of any use. I'd like to see the centre for myself so that I'll know whether to recommend it to other patients. I could see how Jamie copes with the activities and perhaps give you some advice along the way.'

Mrs Brannigan's eyes lit up. 'Would you really be prepared to do that for us? It's such a lot to ask of you, but it would make me feel so much easier in my mind if I knew that you were going to be there, too. You've been so good, explaining Jamie's condition to us and helping us through this. I'd probably be able to cope with the rest of the stay by myself once we had managed the first few days.'

Connor glanced at the boy's father. 'How do you feel about that?'

The man smiled. 'I would certainly feel a lot easier in my mind, knowing that a doctor was going along with my boy. Are you sure that we wouldn't be putting you out too much?'

'Not at all,' Connor said. He hesitated, a brief look of uncertainty crossing his features. 'Of course, you have to bear in mind that I don't have any experience of the centre myself, and I wouldn't want to put you wrong on that score. Dr Linwood here is the expert on that, and I know she volunteered there from time to time. In fact, I had an idea she still does occasionally.' He sent Phoebe a vaguely questioning look, as though he was floundering a touch.

For her part, Phoebe was surprised that Connor knew any of that. She hadn't told him about her stint at the centre, and he wouldn't have heard it from her parents, since they still had their doubts about him. Of course, he had kept in touch with her sister over the years, hadn't he? But why was he showing signs of uncertainty? That wasn't at all like him. Maybe he was concerned for this young boy.

When she remained silent, thinking things through, Connor told the boy's parents, 'I can help you out with Jamie's medical condition, but Phoebe is the one who knows all there is to know about whether the activities might be suitable. She would be the best one to guide you on that score.'

Mrs Brannigan turned to Phoebe. 'Really? Is it true? Do you still volunteer at the centre? It would be wonderful if you could be there with us, too.' Her husband cleared his throat in warning and she pulled herself up, looking flustered all at once. 'Of course, I expect you're much too busy. You must forget I asked. I don't know what I was thinking.'

Jamie's mouth drooped unhappily, and now Phoebe was the one to be uncertain. 'No, that's quite all right. It's true what Dr Broughton was saying, I used to volunteer there on a regular basis. They did so much to help my young niece while she was recovering from various operations and procedures.' She was thoughtful for a moment, disturbed by the sad look in the boy's eyes. 'I dare say I could fit in another weekend there. The organisers are always asking me if I'll go back.'

All at once, Jamie was beaming from ear to ear. 'So I get to go away after all? That's super-cool.'

Jamie and his parents talked to one another excitedly, already making plans for the coming event.

It was only when Phoebe turned away and saw Connor's lips make a faint curve of satisfaction that she realised how neatly she had been manoeuvred into volunteering her services.

Had she really thought he was unsure of himself? What possessed her to think that way? Connor never had doubts. He had led her down the path and held out the bait of the boy's desperate longing so that she would enter the trap willingly.

'Thank you so much for this,' Mrs Brannigan

said, her face wreathed in smiles. 'I'll ring the centre and say that we'll go ahead with the booking.'

The woman turned away and started an animated conversation with her husband and son once more.

Phoebe felt the door of the trap clang firmly into place. She sent Connor a brief, quizzical look, and he returned it with a bland gaze, as though he was innocence itself.

'You said you had some papers for me to sign?' he murmured.

'That's right, I did. I can't think what made me forget.' Her blue eyes lanced into him, and the wretched man dared to smile.

'You've always been extremely good with children,' he murmured in an undertone as he signed the papers, 'no matter much how you doubt yourself. Emily's come a long way since her unfortunate start, and now you would hardly know that there's anything wrong with her. That has to be down to the care she's received over the years from both the medical profession and her family…including her favourite aunt. It'll do you good to go away for the weekend, you'll see. It will help you to see the positive side of things.'

She gave a brief, taut smile in return as she took the papers from him. 'You are in so much trouble,' she muttered. 'Just wait till I get you on your own.'

CHAPTER FIVE

'Is it safe to come in here?' Connor poked his head around the door of the neonatal unit, and caught Phoebe's gaze.

She glowered at him. 'If we didn't have to work together to transport this baby to Somerset, I'd answer that by aiming a barrage of squashed tomatoes at you,' she said in a pithy tone. 'You manipulated the situation with Jamie's parents—don't think that I don't know that.'

He tried to look sheepish and failed dismally. 'I was sort of hoping you might be over that now that you've had an hour or so to cool down.'

'Not a bit of it. There's no way you're off the hook. I've had time to brood over what you did and I've come up with ways of making you pay.'

'Uh-oh. That sounds ominous.' He made as if to back away. 'Maybe I ought to go back down to A and E?'

'Don't even think about it.' Her eyes narrowed on him, her blue gaze becoming smoky. 'I'll sort you out later. In the meantime, the ambulance is ready and waiting and we're all geared up to go.'

'Ah, well, in that case…I suppose I don't really have much of a choice, do I?' He opened the door wider and walked in, ducking and giving an exaggerated glance around as though to avoid any flying missiles. 'How is the baby doing?'

Phoebe sobered. 'Not so good, I'm afraid. I'm worried about her—because of the trauma she went through coming into the world she has a number of problems, not least the fact that her kidneys might fail.'

He made a face. 'That's definitely a complication she could do without, but the hospital she's going to has expertise in dealing with those kinds of problems, doesn't it?' He glanced at the baby who Phoebe had placed in the specialised mobile unit that would protect her during the journey. 'I wonder how the parents feel about all this? It must be terrible for them, being incapacitated themselves. How are they? Are they off the danger list yet?'

She shook her head. 'Not so far. Alex reckons the mother is still very ill, but she's responsive enough to know that her baby is being taken to another hospital. I've spoken to her and told her that as soon as she's well enough she'll be able to stay with the baby. She says they want to call her Sarah.'

Connor made a quick smile. 'That's good. It means she's formed a bond with her, then, despite everything. It's never satisfactory when mother and baby are separated. And what about the father…what state is he in? I heard he had suffered a chest injury and had to undergo heart surgery. Is there any news of him?'

Phoebe was busy gathering together all the documentation that was to go with the baby on the journey, but she glanced at him briefly.

'Jessica reckons he's still under sedation. The consultant is quite worried about him.'

'I can imagine.' He grimaced. 'Well, we'd better do our bit and make sure that baby Sarah comes through this all right, hadn't we? At least she'll have the best care we can give her, with all the state-of-the-art specialised equipment and ventilatory support. Let's make a start, shall we?'

Phoebe nodded, and made a quick check of the baby's heart rate and blood-gas levels. 'Okay. She's as stable as we can manage for now.'

They wheeled her out to the waiting ambulance and spent some time making sure that all was in order as they transferred her into the vehicle.

'How long do you think it will take us to get to the children's hospital?' Phoebe asked the driver after they had secured the transport unit in place.

'Around an hour and a half, I should think.' He glanced at the baby in the incubator and smiled. 'She looks peaceful enough, doesn't she? It always amazes me how tiny they are. Their little heads are covered with bonnets that would hardly stretch over a mushroom.'

The baby wriggled and moved her tiny hand against her cheek as though seeking to suck on her fist. She yawned and her legs trembled a little before settling back into place against her tummy. Phoebe slid a hand inside the incubator and delicately stroked a finger along the baby's arm, marvelling at the softness of her skin. This was such a precious bundle and she desperately wanted her to thrive.

She straightened and glanced back at the driver. 'She came into the world early and she's been through an awful lot in her first few days.'

'I know.' He nodded. 'I'll make it a slow and steady drive, don't you worry. You just keep an eye on the little mite.'

Phoebe's mouth curved. 'I will...but she has Connor to keep her company as well. Between us we should be able to ensure a safe journey.'

She sincerely hoped that was going to be the case, but she couldn't help feeling a tremor of apprehension. Once the driver had secured the doors, he started up the engine and they set off along the road.

She and Connor each settled to their individual roles. Phoebe kept watch on the monitors and adjusted the various fluid lines and drips, while Connor checked the baby's nasogastric tube and applied suction where necessary to keep the area clear.

'She seems to be doing all right so far,' he announced when they had been travelling for around three quarters of an hour.

Phoebe nodded and relaxed a little, glancing out of the window at the rolling countryside. They were crossing Exmoor and the moorland heather spread out like a rich blanket of purple, lilac and yellow. In the distance she could see the rugged coastline where the blue waters of the Bristol Channel lapped at the shore.

'It's beautiful, isn't it?' Connor murmured, following her gaze.

'Yes.' Her mouth softened. 'I've always loved

the scenery around this part of the coast, especially the boats in the harbours. The seashore always has a soothing effect on me and helps to make me feel tranquil.'

'The countryside around here has a lot going for it as well, don't you think?' He pointed out the line of the river, burbling its way through the hills and valleys towards the sea. 'I used to love going for walks along the banks of the river near my home. I'd go with my friends along to the packhorse bridge and we'd hang out amongst the trees and generally waste hours in the summertime, messing about.'

'I remember,' she said. 'There was a special place that you would go to from time to time, wasn't there? It wasn't too far from the headland, a mile or so from the woodland near your house. There were gnarled old trees, I recall, in a small copse, where the river meandered and you could walk out onto a small wooden landing stage.'

'How did you know about that?' he asked,

looking at her curiously. 'I thought that was my hideout, known only to me.'

She gave a brief, secretive smile. 'How did you know about my volunteering at the activity centre?' she countered. 'Did Amy tell you? I know that my sister kept in touch with you after you went to London.'

'We met up from time to time when she brought Emily to the hospital where I was working.' His mouth made a wry shape. 'I think she felt sorry for me, being the village miscreant, and she might have had the idea that I'd been sorely misjudged.'

'Misjudged…hah.' She eyed him scornfully. 'That's a good one. Still, my sister's a great one for listening and sorting out the world's ills.' Phoebe's blue eyes softened. 'Though I recall she said you had been a great help to her when Emily was so poorly. She said you gave her some good advice.'

'I hope it was useful. I was actually working in Cardiology back then, when Emily was due to have her first surgery.'

'Oh, I see. That explains things. It must have been a comfort to her to be able to talk to you.'

'Possibly.'

Phoebe frowned. 'So, if you know all about me being at the activity centre, she must have filled you in on what I was up to from time to time?'

'Occasionally. Though I must admit I found out about your volunteer activities from Mr Kirk.'

'From Mr Kirk?' Her brows shot up. 'I don't think I follow you. Why on earth would Mr Kirk tell you about that? I'm not even on his team.'

'No, but he said you were in the department for a short time, on a colleague's team. He had some dealings with the people who run the centre, apparently, as his patients go to stay there from time to time, and he was quite impressed with what they had to say about how helpful you were. I think he has a good opinion of you in general and he'd been hoping that you would apply to work in Cardiac Care.'

'Heavens.' She blinked. 'I hadn't realised. That's useful to know for when I have to decide where to apply for my next training rotation.' She sent him a puzzled look. 'But I still don't see why he would tell you any of that.'

His expression was rueful. 'It's probably because I got up his nose, as you put it the other day. I had to refer a child for cardiac surgery, and I suggested to him that we should be making better use of the operating theatres. As you pointed out, it didn't go down too well with him. In fact, he seemed quite affronted.'

She winced. 'I can imagine.'

'Then when I mentioned that I was thinking of bringing in a business guru to explain to management how we could achieve higher quotas he told me I should find ways of making better use of all this spare time I seemed to have. Why didn't I do as you had done, he said, and occupy myself by volunteering my services in other areas? Then I wouldn't be so prone to stir up trouble?'

Phoebe shook her head in dismay. 'You never learn, do you? You have everything going for you, and yet you still manage to go and put a spoke in your own wheel.'

He laughed. 'You're right…but I hate to see wasted opportunity. Things could be so much better if people would accept the notion of change from time to time instead of sticking their heads in the sand.'

Just then the monitors began to bleep and they both hurried to find out what had set them off. The baby was squirming a little, appearing faintly distressed, and among other problems the heart monitor was indicating signs of cardiac excitability.

'Her kidney function is failing,' Phoebe said anxiously. 'I'll give her medication to compensate, and hope that things settle down.' She prepared the infusion. 'I wonder if we should look again at the ventilation?'

'I'll see to it. I'll adjust the rate.'

They both worked quickly to restore the balance of the baby's blood chemistry, and after a while, when the monitors stopped bleeping and the infant was peaceful once more, Phoebe cautiously settled back in her seat.

'I think she's over the worst, for the moment. I hope they'll be able to sort out all her problems at the hospital she's going to. I've become really fond of her over these last few days, and I couldn't bear it if anything bad was to happen to her.'

'They have renal specialists there, and I'm sure the consultant will give her the very best attention.'

'Yes, I know you're right. It's just…I'm letting myself become too involved.' She pulled herself together and sent him a wondering look. 'I still can't believe you had the nerve to challenge a top consultant about his working practices. What were you thinking?'

He shrugged. 'If you don't try, you'll never get anywhere, will you? At least, that's my philosophy.' He looked her over for a moment, his thoughts obviously roaming elsewhere. 'That's why I…' But then he stopped speaking and Phoebe sent him a questioning glance.

'That's why you…what?'

'Nothing. Forget I said anything.' He straightened, as though mentally bringing himself under control, and then he checked the baby in the incubator once more. 'You said earlier that you had been brooding over this business of the activity centre. So what fiendish plan have you thought up to make me pay for involving you?'

'Hah…worried now, aren't you?' She threw him a jubilant look. 'Well, since you're going to be taking up my leisure time, I decided I might as well take up yours in turn.'

'Really? Is that a promise? I think I like the sound of that.' His eyes took on a gleam of mischief and he edged closer to her. 'Tell me more. I always thought we could spark a firework display if ever we were to get together.'

'Back off,' she said, fixing him with a laser-sharp gaze. 'It's a pity you can't go and take a cold shower.'

He shook his head. 'You don't mean that. You're just playing hard to get, aren't you?'

She smiled at him sweetly. 'There's no playfulness about it,' she murmured. 'I'm deadly serious. You don't stand a chance, not a smidgen, zilch. You're about as likely to get close to me as you are to be Mr Kirk's right-hand man.'

'Ouch. That really hurt. I'm crushed.' His expression was pained, and Phoebe laughed.

'Yeah. Sure you are. Pull the other one.' She looked at the baby and checked the monitors. When she had reassured herself that all was well, she turned back to him and said, 'The thing is, I've had an idea for raising funds for the neonatal unit. We always need more equipment, and it would be great if we could expand the unit so that we could treat more babies.'

He raised his brows. 'That sounds as though you're becoming protective of the little ones in your care. I thought you had your mind set against being a children's doctor?'

'Well, yes, but it isn't that.' Phoebe checked the monitors once more and noted down the results on her observation sheet. Thankfully, the baby seemed to have suffered no ill effects from the earlier problems. 'It's just that they do such good work in the unit, and even if I can't be the one to stay there and work with them, I could do something to help.' She fixed him with a direct look. 'Or you can, by working with me to set this up.'

'Set what up? What are we talking about?'

'A sponsored walk.'

He was unimpressed. 'Well, that's not going to raise a whole lot of money, is it? You'd have to get half the hospital involved to get anywhere near the amount you'd need.'

'We'll work on that. Stop being such a wet blanket. Anyway, you don't have any choice but to agree. I've made up my mind. I told you, I've been brooding on this.'

'Scheming, more like.'

She glowered at him. 'And then there's the raffle to organise… And I thought a barbecue would go down well in the evening. We could charge an entrance fee or simply add a bit on to the cost of the food.'

'And I'm supposed to help with all this?' He

raised dark brows. 'You're a hard taskmaster. I'd say there was a bit more than two days' worth of effort involved there, wouldn't you?'

'And why not? Let it teach you a lesson.'

They might have gone on with the banter, except that the ambulance came to a halt and the driver cut the engine. They both realised that they must have reached their destination at last.

The driver came to open up the doors of the vehicle, and between them they brought the baby out of the ambulance and wheeled her into the hospital. A team was waiting to receive her, and Phoebe handed over all the paperwork that travelled along with the infant, while Connor talked to the consultant about the baby's case notes.

'Thanks for all this,' the consultant said, doing a swift check of the baby and assessing the state of the monitor readings. 'We'll take it from here,' she said. 'Do you want to take a break for an hour or so while we look her over? That way, if we need any more input from you, we could perhaps get back to you before you make the return journey. Sometimes things crop up that we might not have planned for, and it would be easier to deal with them if the transfer team is still around.'

'That sounds fine to me,' Connor murmured, sending a swift glance towards Phoebe. She nodded acknowledgement and he continued, 'Our driver has gone off to find himself something to eat, so we'll be around here for a while longer.' He gave the doctor his mobile number.

'Thanks. You might like to wander around the hospital gardens for a while. There's an arboretum on the east side of the building, with terraced areas and a lily pond, and there are picnic tables where you can sit and eat lunch, if you like.'

'That sounds like a pleasant way to while away an hour,' Phoebe said.

They found their way to the hospital restaurant and bought crusty salad rolls and fruit buns for lunch, with cold drinks to wash them down. The driver was talking to a fellow ambulanceman, but he waved acknowledgement when they indicated that they were going outside.

'So who was this guru that you wanted to bring into the hospital?' Phoebe asked as they walked along the path to the wooded area.

'He's someone I met in London, a friend who works in the City. Essentially he's a troubleshooter, but he also acted as a financial advisor to me once I made up my mind to go to medical school.'

She lifted a brow. 'I'm surprised by that. I thought your father knew all there was to know about running a successful business. I'd have thought he would be the first person you would turn to.'

He made a wry face. 'You know how my father is…ebullient at the best of times, and way too busy with sorting out his own problems to be bothered concerning himself with much of anything else. As for turning to him for help and advice, I gave up doing that a long time ago. My father believed you should make your own decisions and stand by them. As for me, I obviously made all the wrong choices and he clearly thought I'd never amount to anything.'

He stopped and indicated a secondary path that led to a leafy arbour. 'I think we need to go this way.'

She followed him and frowned. 'I know you were often at odds with your father as a boy, but perhaps back then he had good reason to be annoyed with you. You were always flouting the rules. He must see that you're not the same nowadays. You're doing a worthwhile job, and people respect you. Even I can see that you're not the person you were.'

He clutched a hand to his heart. 'Am I hearing things right? You see something in me other than a rabble-rouser and troublemaker? Wonders will never cease. I've waited a long time for that one to happen.'

She laughed. 'Can you blame me for taking a while to come round? If your own father had doubts about you, what do you expect?'

They came across a clearing in the trees, where rough-hewn terraces had been laid out, and bench tables were set out at intervals on the grass. Further away, there was a pond, edged with reeds and aquatic plants.

'Hmm. I suppose you may be right.' He frowned. 'I did give him a hard time, didn't I?' He went over to a table that was lit by a pool of warm sunlight. 'Shall we sit here and eat? It looks as though we have the place to ourselves, and this seems to be the best spot.'

She nodded, sliding onto a bench seat and laying the food out on the table. Connor placed the cold drinks on the wooden slats and slipped into place beside her so that they were both looking out over the pond. Lily pads floated on the surface of the water, their flowers opened up in shades of pink and white.

She bit into her crusty roll. 'I think the worst must have been when you took your father's car from the garage and started racing with the boys from the village. Word got out that you were all racketing up and down the old disused airfield, and I was worried sick in case anyone ended up hurt. I kept thinking there was going to be the worst kind of trouble when your father found out.'

He began to eat, demolishing the bread as though he was starving. 'We were young and reckless.'

She looked at him. 'I was right, though, wasn't I? I just knew that when your father came home there would be the row to end all rows.'

'It's true.' An expression of guilt washed over his face. 'I pranged the car because I took a bend too fast, and I ended up hitting one of the barricades. I smacked my head on the dashboard because I wasn't wearing a seat belt, and I twisted the ligaments in my arm trying to wrench the car back on track.'

He grimaced, remembering. 'It was complete and utter madness. I was seventeen and I'd just passed my driving test. Somehow, even though I knew I deserved punishment because I took the car and made a mess of it, I wasn't expecting my father's furious reaction. I thought he would appreciate that I'd come off the worse for wear and realise that it might have taught me a lesson.'

'That didn't happen, though, did it?' Her eyes were troubled as she studied him. What was it that possessed him to go against everyone and everything? Wasn't he still doing the same, by setting himself up against the cardiac consultant?

'No. He read me the Riot Act and promised all kinds of retribution that he would bring down on my head. It made me angry that he seemed to care more about the car than he did for me, and I stormed out of the house threatening to never come back.'

'Heaven knows what your mother must have thought.' Phoebe remembered that day as though it was imprinted on her mind in flame. 'No one knew where you had gone, and even though they sent people out looking for you, they didn't find you. I was beside myself wondering if you were wandering about concussed, or lying in a ditch somewhere suffering from hypothermia.'

He tilted his head on one side, looking at her. 'Were you? I was so wrapped up in myself I didn't give a thought for anybody else and what they might be thinking. If I'd known that you were looking for me, things might have turned out differently.'

She shook her head. 'I doubt that. You didn't give a jot about what any of us thought. You didn't tell anyone where you were going.'

'It's true.' He made a wry face. 'I wanted to be alone to rage against the world in general and show my bitterness against unfeeling, heavy-handed parents. I was a poor, misunderstood youth, on the verge of manhood, and I thought it would serve them right if they never saw me again.' He sent her a curious glance. 'Were you really worried?'

She nodded. 'I searched everywhere, in all the places where I thought you might have hidden yourself away, but I drew a blank everywhere.' She knew that he would have done the same for her back then. Alex had been the one who had looked out for her, but so did Connor. Maybe it was because she was young and she tended to hang around with his cousin and he had felt obligated whenever Alex hadn't been around. Whatever the reason, he had been protective towards her, and she had felt concerned for him, too.

'I couldn't imagine what must have been going through your head, and my mood kept swinging between wanting to tell you what a mess you were making of things and wanting to comfort you and make everything right again.'

His mouth softened. 'Not much of a change there, then.' His eyes glimmered. 'You still hover on the brink between exasperation and caring for me, don't you? Go on, admit it.'

'I won't. You're a pain in the neck, Connor. You always have been and you'll probably stay that way for ever.'

He put an arm around her shoulders and drew her to him. 'But despite all that, you do care for me, just a teensy bit, don't you?'

'I'm not admitting to anything. You drive me to distraction.'

'I'll settle for that,' he murmured, 'for the time being, at least. Distracted is good. I like distracted.' Slowly, he lowered his head until his cheek was just a breath away from hers, and then, before she had time to take on board what he was about, he was kissing her, softly, tenderly, his lips brushing hers and exploring the curving line of her mouth.

The kiss was like a lick of flame gliding along her nerve endings. Heat built up in her, engulfing her, taking her over so that she could think of nothing but the sheer ecstasy of that moment. His warmth, the feel of his body close to hers, his arms sliding around her and drawing her to him, were all sensations she had never known before, and it was a dizzying experience, one that took hold of her and wrapped her in a comforting mist of heady delight.

Everything went out of her head. There was only the sweet sound of birdsong all around and the feel of the sun's rays glancing along her arms. It all felt so right, so perfect, so exhilarating, as though this was all completely natural, the only satisfactory end to them being together.

And yet…as a light breeze riffled through the trees, soft whispers of doubt echoed in her mind. This was Connor, a man at odds with the world around him, a restless spirit who never stayed in one place for more than a year or so, who turned on the charm as though it lived and breathed within him.

He would play fast and loose with her affections, and make fun of her indecision. Why was she doing this? Why was she letting him weave a spell around her?

For that's what it was, a dreamlike, enchanted moment that would soon be lost in the mists of time. It wasn't real.

She drew back from Connor, looking at him with bemusement in her eyes.

'Are you okay?' he asked.

'I don't know.' She was floundering, her nervous system firing off sparks as though he had inadvertently lit a fuse in her. 'I think I'm confused. What was that all about?'

'I'm not altogether sure.' He gave her a faint

smile. 'It seemed like a good idea at the time. Don't you think so?'

'I don't know what I think. My mind's gone into freefall.'

He smiled. 'Shall I kiss you again and see if things become any clearer?'

He moved towards her once more and she put up a hand to fend him off. 'I think maybe you'd better not.'

He made a rueful face. 'Is this because of Alex? He's always on your mind in one way or another, isn't he? Sometimes I think I'd very much like to change that.'

'But you won't.' She shook her head. Alex, after all, was someone she could rely on. He was her best friend, her confidant, and he was always there for her. She couldn't be sure that Alex loved her, but her affections had always been focussed on him, and it was as though she was being disloyal to him by allowing Connor to get close to her this way. 'I won't let you play havoc with my emotions the way you do with everyone else. I told you, I'm immune.'

'Hmm.' He studied her for a second or two. 'That might not last for ever, you know. You might think you're protected for all time, but eventually the defences break down and you find that you're not as resistant as you thought you were.'

She gave a soft, shuddery sigh. 'So you think you can win me over, do you?' Her heart clicked into a rapid, chaotic beat at the very thought. 'That just confirms what I suspected all along. You have no conscience. You're like an infection, a kind of virus that slips into place undercover and threatens to take over the whole system.' She shook her head. 'It's not going to happen. I'm forewarned and armed for action.'

He made a wry face. 'I knew I should have gone slower, but you looked so sweet and it blew my mind that you cared enough to worry about me, even way back when we were young.' He sent her a thoughtful glance. 'Could I persuade you that I'm in dire straits now and in need of cosseting?'

She didn't answer, but her eyes narrowed on him, shooting a warning volley.

'No? Ah, well, forget I mentioned it.' He gave a resigned sigh and started to gather up the remains of their al fresco lunch. 'I dare say we should be getting back to work anyway.'

CHAPTER SIX

PHOEBE cradled the baby in her arms. Everything about the infant was perfect, from the downy, rose-tinted skin to her beautifully formed fingers and toes.

'She's delightful,' she said, looking at the child's mother. 'You must be so proud to be taking her home.'

'I am. She was so tiny when she was born, and it was upsetting to see her struggling for every breath…and yet to look at her now you wouldn't know what she had been through, would you? I'm really grateful to you for all that you've done. Everyone here has been so good to us.'

'It's great for us to know that your baby is doing

so well. It's what we're here for, to make sure that they have the best care we can give them.'

Carefully, Phoebe handed the baby over to the mother, who nestled the infant in her arms and tenderly adjusted the shawl around the infant's soft, dimpled cheeks. Her husband looked on and slid a supportive arm around his wife's waist, before leading her towards the exit.

Phoebe watched them go, feeling happy for the small family, and when the door closed behind them, Jessica came out from the office to claim her attention. 'It's lovely to see the babies when they're ready to go home, isn't it?' she murmured.

'It is. That little one was premature and needed support on the ventilator for a while, but she's coping well with breathing now on her own.'

Jessica nodded. 'So is that you finished for the day?'

Phoebe nodded. 'That's right. I have to go and meet Connor down in Reception. He's driving us to the activity centre for the weekend.'

'Yes, I saw him loading your overnight bag

into the car this morning. That's why I dropped by…to say cheerio, and wish you well, and tell you not to do anything that I wouldn't do.'

'Mmm…that gives me a fair amount of leeway, doesn't it?' Phoebe grinned as Jessica pretended to be affronted.

'Huh…I wish. I'm too busy trying to keep up with Mr Kirk's work schedule to have time for any shenanigans,' she said. 'He's very thorough, and he expects me to keep on top of everything. It's difficult, because he has such a heavy workload, but he's brilliant and I'm learning so much.'

'That's something, at least.' Phoebe grimaced. 'Alex is finding things hard going, too, at the moment. We spent a few hours the other evening, going through some of the notes he had missed from his training afternoons. He's worried about his upcoming review.'

Jessica smiled. 'And then you finished off down the pub…I saw you both shooting off out around ten o'clock. I'd have gone with you if it hadn't been for me having to do a stint on night shift. Did you run into Connor while you were there? He said he might drop by.'

Phoebe shook her head. 'No. I didn't realise he was around. I thought he was with Lisa from A and E. She said he was helping her move furniture into her new house.' She didn't know what to make of that, and it bothered her to think about Connor and Lisa. Was there something going on between the two of them? After all, as Alex had pointed out, he hadn't come home the other night, and the two of them were very chatty whenever she saw them together.

'Yes, I wondered about that.' Jessica frowned. 'Of course they work together, but they seem to be keeping company away from the hospital quite a bit, too. Makes me wonder if something's going on there.' Her eyes widened. 'Connor's never going to be short of women friends, is he? They all seem to want to get to know him better.'

'You could be right. That's always been the way.'

Why, then, had he kissed her when they had

been in the arboretum? Her cheeks burned at the memory, and a feverish thrill of guilt ran through her. The kiss had come out of the blue, and Connor was the last person she should be daydreaming about, yet those few tender moments would stay with her for ever.

But perhaps he had simply been making the most of an opportunity when it had presented itself. That surely was the only explanation. It rankled, but there wasn't much she could do about it except remind herself not to make the same mistake again. She needed to keep a barrier in place between them.

Connor was a complex character, and he had intrigued her from the moment she had first met him, all those years ago. He wasn't the staying kind, though, and any woman who allowed herself to fall for him could easily be hurt.

Besides, Alex was the one who made her feel special. They had been friends since way back, and all she wanted from him was some indication that he might one day fall in love with her.

For a long time now she had looked on him as the one man she might want to be with for the rest of her life.

'Anyway,' Jessica murmured, 'it'll probably do you good to go away for a couple of days. You've been anxious about all these babies in your care, and being with older children for a while might help you to put things in perspective…see how they cope with their problems. Mostly they become stronger as they grow, and the centre is a kind of convalescence for them, isn't it?'

'I suppose it is. I know Emily loved being there and she hasn't looked back since.'

'There you are, then. Go enjoy yourself. You have a way with children, and I can't see you as anything other than a children's doctor. I don't know why you have so many doubts.'

'Now you sound like Connor.' Phoebe gave a wry smile. 'Save me from people who think they know my mind better than I do.'

'Off with you,' Jessica said. 'I have to go back down to Cardiology, and you need to get a life.'

'Yeah, right. As if the same doesn't apply to you, too.'

Jessica laughed, and the two women made their way down to Reception, where Connor was standing by the desk, chatting to the clerk on duty.

'There you are,' he said, taking his leave of the girl at the desk with a smile and a lift of his hand. He walked towards them, his gaze moving over Phoebe. 'I was about to send out a search party. The evening meal's at six o'clock, and I'd be well miffed if I missed out on the beefsteak pie.'

'Your appetite will be the end of you,' Jessica murmured, throwing him a quick grin. 'Still, judging from the energy you put into everything, you need to keep up your strength, don't you?' She sent a swift glance in the direction of the clerk, and Connor's mouth twisted.

'I'm misjudged and maligned wherever I go.'

'Sure you are.' Jessica turned to Phoebe. 'Have a great time. Don't let the children overwhelm you with worrying about them…and Alex sends his love. He said he wishes he were going with you.'

'I bet he does.' Phoebe smiled. 'He just fancies a spot of canoeing, if the truth be known.'

They parted company, Jessica walking off towards the cardiology department while Connor and Phoebe headed for the car park.

'I think Alex has more on his mind than watersports,' Connor murmured as they went out into the fresh air. 'I spoke to him this afternoon, and he seemed quite concerned for your well-being. He seems to think you're going to find this trip difficult. I'm pretty sure he's bothered by the idea of you and I being together for a couple of days, but there's more to it than that. He said you were troubled last time you stayed at the centre.'

They reached his car, and Connor pulled open the passenger side door for her. Phoebe slid into her seat and buckled up, the scent of new leather upholstery teasing her nostrils. She leaned back and stretched out her legs, marvelling for a minute or two at the comfort and luxury of the car.

'I was worried about a child who was staying there,' she said quietly as he came and sat behind the wheel. 'She wasn't very strong, and it upset me to see her struggle. I think that was what finally decided me that I wasn't going to work with children when I've completed my senior house officer years.'

'And yet you went against your better judgement to go there again.' He sent her a brief, appreciative look. 'I think that shows you have courage and compassion and the will to help youngsters.'

'It means I'm a weak fool,' she said, pulling a rueful face.

He started the engine. 'Not a bit of it.' He gave her another oblique glance. 'Otherwise you'd have given in and succumbed to all my overtures, past and present, whereas instead you've resolutely pushed me away.' He shook his head. 'That strikes me as a woman of determination.' He smiled wryly. 'Loyal, too, though I never did fully understand what it is that you and Alex have going on between you. You're not a couple, are you?'

She didn't answer right away and he concentrated on driving out of the hospital grounds, turning the car on to the North West road.

'Alex has always been good to me,' she said eventually. 'He helped me make up my mind what it was I wanted when Emily was so ill, and it was because he talked me through all the options that I realised I wanted to study medicine.'

She let her gaze dwell on Connor for a while, watching his calm, smooth manner behind the wheel. His hands were strong and capable, with a light touch but one that was definitely in control the whole time. He knew exactly what it was that he wanted, and what he was about, and she guessed it was all the frustration and rebellion of his youth that had forged him into the man he was today.

She, on the other hand, had blown with the wind, unsure of herself, concerned about what was for the best if she was to help others, and dithering about the path she should take.

'That wasn't all of it, though, was it?' he commented. 'We've all four of us talked about what we wanted to do with our lives. None of us was certain to begin with.'

'Maybe not. But Alex helped me to find a place to stay when I started out at medical school, and he looked out for me all the time. He knew when I was having a hard time, and he took care of me. I feel as though I owe him a lot.'

'You can't build a relationship on gratitude.' His tone had a mocking edge. 'Otherwise we'd all be hugging one another and swearing undying love.'

Her gaze pinioned him. 'You're so shallow,' she said. 'Alex watched over me when I first left the family home. He was there for me when I had a bad bout of flu, and he bolstered me up when I was worried about exams.'

'You mean he told you to put your books away and get out in the sunshine,' Connor retorted. 'Alex believes in taking breaks when things get too much, and his priorities are geared up to what's relevant to him at the time.' He flicked her a glance. 'Besides, I'd have come and mopped your brow if I'd known you were ill.'

'From what your cousin reported, you were too busy celebrating passing your finals by absconding with the skeletons from the lecture hall. I heard they were seen on the roof of the hospital, dressed in dinner suits and gowns and partying with champagne and wineglasses.'

He chuckled. 'What can I say? No one could actually prove who was responsible, could they? The dean might have expressed his disapproval for such antics, but apart from reprimanding the whole student fraternity there wasn't much else he could do. Besides, we returned them to the lecture hall in due course. No harm was done.'

He turned the car on to the Exmoor road and sent her a sideways glance. 'Seriously, though, if I'd known you were ill, I would have been there with you. You could have phoned me. I'd have come right away.'

'I'd hardly do that, would I? You were in London and I hadn't seen you in years. Anyway, there was no need. I didn't even tell my parents. Alex stayed with me and Jessica came over whenever she was free.'

'I see what I'm up against.' His mouth made a wry shape. 'The odds are overwhelming. I never stood a chance, did I?'

She sent him a sweet smile and reached out to pat his hand. 'You'll get over it,' she murmured. 'I heard that fickle was your middle name.'

Touching him was a big mistake, she discovered. His long fingers were relaxed on the gear lever, lightly tanned, strong and supple, while his wrists were hard boned, totally masculine, the sunlight glinting on faint golden hairs. It was almost like a ripple effect, the way the energy passed from him to her. It ricocheted along her arm and through her body, filling her with heat and strange sensations that were wholly new to her.

He glanced at her, as though he felt it, too, but he stayed silent and she quickly put her hand back in her lap where it belonged. What was she thinking of, stroking the tiger in his den? Of course she had imagined his reaction. She was the one with the trigger reflexes, not him. He was cool and in control of himself, as always. The days of the reckless, troubled teenager were long past.

They arrived at the centre in under half an hour. Phoebe was calmer by then, and her brief moment of uncertainty had passed. Connor insisted on carrying their bags into the building, and together they went to Reception to find out where they would be staying for the next two nights.

'I've put you both in the barn conversion,' the receptionist told them. 'It's self-contained, with two bedrooms and en suite bathrooms upstairs, and a kitchen and living room downstairs, so you should have pretty much everything you need in there. Of course, you can have meals in the res- taurant if you don't want to fend for yourselves.'

'That sounds wonderful,' Phoebe told her. 'It's good that we still have an hour left to settle in before the evening meal.' She made a slight frown. 'Do you know whether Mrs Brannigan and her son have arrived yet?'

'I think they were running a bit late,' the woman told her. 'She rang to ask us to set some supper aside for them.'

'Okay, thanks. We'll catch up with them later.'

They found the barn conversion in a secluded spot on the periphery of the centre. It was built of stone, with a deeply sloping roof that had window panels set into it at intervals. Connor unlocked the door, ushering her inside, before stepping in and placing the overnight bags down on the tiled floor of the wide hall.

'This looks good,' he said, glancing around. 'First impressions, and all that. It's very light and spacious—though I expect you're already familiar with this place, aren't you?'

'I'm not,' she said, walking through to the sitting room and glancing around. 'I think this conversion must be new.' She turned and beckoned him. 'Come and look at this, it's lovely. There's a window seat, looking out over the lawn, and there's even a paved area where you can sit outside.'

He came and stood next to her, laying a hand lightly on her shoulder. 'It's very pretty,' he murmured. He looked at her, his glance drifting over her and settling briefly on her hair, her cheekbones and the curving line of her throat.

She sent him a brief, uncertain look, and he broke the connection, surveying the room and pausing for a while to take it all in.

Phoebe realised that she was holding her breath. With his hand on her shoulder she couldn't think straight, and his nearness was having a very strange effect on her, causing her heartbeat to change gear from slow and steady to ultra-fast in the blink of an eye. Somehow in these new surroundings her responses were more intense.

After a moment, though, he took a step back from her and turned away. 'I'll take the bags upstairs. Do you want to come and look at the rooms?'

She nodded, pulling in a swift breath as she gave a final glance around before following him.

The upstairs accommodation was finished to

the same high standard as the ground floor. The bedrooms had been fitted in under the eaves, but they were spacious and filled with sunshine that poured in through the skylights.

'That's something I hadn't expected,' he said, looking towards glass doors that took up a good portion of one wall.

She walked over to them and opened them up. 'Oh, my,' she said, 'there's a balcony out here.' She stepped out onto it and breathed in the country air. 'Just look at that view.'

Connor came and looked out, following her gaze. 'It's beautiful,' he said. 'You can see right out over the valley.'

'It's fantastic,' she agreed. 'I had no idea there was any accommodation like this. I've only ever stayed in the basic self-catering apartments when I've been here before.' She turned to him. 'You must have picked out the best of the bunch.'

'Something like that,' he agreed. 'It occurred to me that if we had somewhere idyllic to stay, you might give up on going out and about, and we could spend the whole weekend here, just the two of us.'

She sent him a harassed smile. 'Sure you did,' she said. 'You wouldn't have spared a thought for the Brannigans being left to their own devices, would you?'

'Well, maybe just a teeny one.' He held up his fingers, demonstrating, as though he was taking a pinch of salt.

'You're hopeless,' she said, shaking her head. 'What am I to do with you?'

'Throw caution to the wind and elope with me,' he suggested, a wicked grin curving his mouth. 'No one will miss us for a while, and I promise to have you back here, safe and sound, at some point. I'm not exactly sure when that would be, but we could think about it eventually.'

'Think about unpacking your bags and getting ready for the evening meal,' she told him firmly. 'As if you'd let anything come between you and a three-course dinner.'

He blinked. 'True. That's very true.' He clapped a hand to his head. 'What on earth was I thinking?'

'I could hazard a guess, but on second thoughts I won't go there. Out of the room, Dr Broughton… this one will do nicely for me. Go play on your own balcony.'

He walked mournfully out of the room, and she could hear his soft mutterings as he went. 'Cruel, hard-hearted woman. Made of stone…has to be. I'm maltreated and misunderstood. Was there ever anyone dealt as bad a hand as me?'

Phoebe's mouth curved. All sorts of adjectives came to mind where Connor was concerned… irrepressible, mischievous, wily and conniving, to name just a few.

He may well tease her and test her mettle, but underneath it all was there just a hint of real intent?

Connor had never been one to let chance pass him by, and for all his artifice and devious ways she couldn't help but feel a tug of attraction towards him. Was she in danger of losing her heart to him?

She couldn't let that happen. He would never seriously entertain the idea of love and commitment, yet those were values she prized above all else.

CHAPTER SEVEN

'OKAY, then. What do we have planned for today?' Connor looked at Jamie across the breakfast table, inviting him to choose. 'There's fishing, canoeing, archery practice or horse riding, to name but a few.'

'I want to try the zip wire,' Jamie said, his eyes shining in anticipation. 'I saw the children whizzing down it last night and I wanted to have a go then, but Mum said no, it was too late, we'd only just got here and we needed to unpack.'

'I noticed them, too,' Phoebe said. 'They looked as though they were having a great time, didn't they?'

Jamie nodded excitedly and started to talk animatedly to Phoebe about everything he wanted to try while he was at the centre. 'And I want to take lots of photos—I got a new camera for my birthday.'

'That's a good idea. What kind is it?'

Seeing that Jamie was deep in conversation, Connor glanced at Mrs Brannigan. 'Whizzing down the zip wire sounds like fun… What do you think, Chloe?'

She looked a little doubtful. 'To be honest,' she said, keeping her voice low so that Jamie would not hear, 'I'm not altogether sure what will be okay for him and what won't.'

Connor nodded. 'Up to now, you've always let him choose his own activities, haven't you? Generally, children with heart problems are very sensible in knowing their own limitations. I think the same probably applies after surgery. Up to now he's made a good recovery, so we're justified in hoping that he'll become stronger and eventually be able to lead a normal life.'

'But he collapsed a while ago… I'm afraid that might happen again.'

'It's understandable that you're worried, and certainly we need to keep an eye on his blood pressure. Having the occasional bout of hypertension doesn't signify that anything major is wrong. It probably just means that he over-extended himself too soon, and he'll learn to adjust to that.'

Jamie finished telling Phoebe about his new camera, and then turned back to his mother. 'So can I go on the wire today? It'll be great. I can't wait to try it out.'

Chloe hesitated, and Jamie directed his plea towards Connor. 'Will you tell her it'll be okay?'

'I think you'll be fine.' He frowned. 'Mind you, your mother said she might like to do some of these things with you, so we do have to bear her old age and infirmity in mind, don't we? She might need some help if she's going to try it with you.' He winked at the boy, and Jamie laughed, looking at his mother to see her reaction.

'Cheeky monkey,' she said, giving Connor a playful punch. 'We'll see who can keep up, just you wait and see.'

Connor shook his head, looking back at Jamie. 'These women are all talk and no substance, don't you think? There was Phoebe telling me she wouldn't even contemplate trying out the archery, and just because I pinched her toast she's getting ready to paint a target on me. You and I will just have to stick together, lad. Men of iron, that's us.'

Jamie giggled. 'You're daft,' he said.

'Never a truer word,' Phoebe put in, glancing up from sipping her orange juice. She looked back at Jamie. 'Of course, once you've had a go on the wire, you might want to try something completely different. We could always go for a wander round the wildlife site. I heard there were some roe deer hiding out among the trees, and all kinds of different birds to see. I know you said you were interested in bird watching. You might like to take some pictures for your photo album.'

Jamie nodded. 'Perhaps we could do that this afternoon. I really want to have a go on the zip wire first. It looks as though it will be fun, shooting down over the trail and going through the trees.'

Connor looked at Jamie's mother. 'Is that okay with you? There's a lift up to the top of the slope. He'll be strapped into a harness—one that supports him in a kind of cradle seat, and then once he's been lifted up to the start point he'll be able to zoom along the wire in comfort. All the children seem to love it.'

Chloe nodded. 'If you think he'll be all right doing that, it's fine with me.'

Jamie gave her a beaming smile, and Phoebe thought how wonderful it was that this young boy had been given his quality of life back after heart surgery. He had been born with a defect to his heart that had made it difficult for his blood to circulate effectively, and as a consequence he had been frail, short of breath a lot of the time, and unable to take part in the normal activities that children of his age enjoyed.

Now, though, he was ready to sample the

delights of outdoor feats that would have debilitated him before his surgery.

'Come on, then, soldier. Let's get moving, shall we?' Connor said. 'We'll possibly need to stop off at the shop, so that your mother can buy her newspaper and a few postcards. That way, your breakfast will have time to settle.'

Jamie frowned. 'Do we have to, Mum? You'll be ages in the shop. You always are.'

'Yes, we do,' his mother said with a wry smile. 'Anyway, you can go and talk to some of the other children while you're waiting for me. Didn't you say there was a boy you met last night that you were going to hang around with? I thought he said he would be near the photo shop first thing?'

'Oh, yes…I forgot. That's okay—take as long as you like in the shop.'

Phoebe smiled. Jamie was a typical boy, wanting to do everything all at once. Connor had been egging him on, but she knew that he had the boy's welfare at heart. He had a medical bag on hand in case the child's heart rhythm changed dramatically, and there was oxygen ready if necessary. She hoped it wouldn't be needed.

'Are you going to have a go?' Connor asked her some half an hour later as they watched Jamie and his mother shoot past them in turn on the wire. Jamie was grinning in delight, and Chloe looked equally thrilled.

'I'm game if you are,' Phoebe said, 'though I have to say this feature is a new addition to the centre and I haven't ever tried it before.'

'You'll be fine. I had a go when I was on holiday in Scotland a couple of years ago, and it's exhilarating.'

Phoebe reserved judgement on that, but she queued up with Connor to use the wire, and when it came to getting into the harness he was there to lend a hand.

'Step into it,' he murmured, 'and I'll do the clasps for you.'

Phoebe had never used this type of harness before, and she accepted his offer of help readily enough, without realising how much intimate contact would be involved. He clipped everything into place, and she was conscious of his every movement, aware of his hands brushing her body, gliding over her jeans-clad legs to ensure that the straps were correctly fitted and shifting to adjust the tension of the bands across her back and chest. He checked the belt around her waist and made sure that the straps were secure around her shoulders.

'Does that feel okay?' he asked, when he had finished.

'Um…yes, thanks,' she managed, keeping her head lowered so that he wouldn't be able to see the pink flush of her cheeks. What had she let herself in for? The slightest touch of his fingers caused every nerve fibre in her body to flare in heated response. This was just the beginning of her stay here. How was she going to cope with having him this close for the next couple of days? Her body was betraying her at every turn.

Riding the wire, when she finally set off on the

downhill run, was a fantastic experience. The speed of the descent gave her an adrenaline rush, and it was good to be out in the open, feeling the soft touch of the breeze on her face and loving the way it rippled through her hair. The scenery all around was breathtakingly beautiful as she swung through the dappled sunlight in the trees and descended into the glorious open space of the valley below.

Connor had gone ahead of her and reached the end of the trail some minutes before she did. As she felt her feet touch the ground he was waiting, ready to steady her and help her to regain her balance just as he had done for Jamie.

'Whoa,' he said, catching hold of her as she began to spin round in a dizzying circle. 'I have hold of you.'

He certainly did. She couldn't be anything but conscious of the way his arms were wrapped around her, and she was fairly sure that her dizziness had nothing whatever to do with her landing. His warm, sure touch had a lot to answer for.

'Are you steady now?'

'I am. Thanks.' She straightened and pulled in a quick breath, knowing that she ought to put some distance between them and at the same time revelling in their closeness. What on earth was wrong with her that she should be feeling this way?

Throughout the rest of the day they moved from one pursuit to another, letting Jamie choose what he wanted to do.

'For a boy who started life with a heart problem, Jamie is definitely making up for lost time,' Phoebe remarked to his mother. 'He seems to have packed so much into today.' They were walking slowly back towards the courtyard shopping area after their evening meal, and Jamie was with another boy, heading for the quad bike circuit just a few yards away.

'You're right. I've been amazed at how he's kept going. Mind you, we've been careful to have restful periods in between. As Connor said, Jamie's chosen those for himself, so he's obviously aware of what he can do and what he can't. I'm just pleased that he hasn't needed to have any extra medication.'

'He might only need this one course of beta blockers to keep the hypertension in check,' Connor murmured. 'He's on a very low dose at the moment. See how he goes over the next day or two. I've had a word with the local doctor, and he'll be on hand to advise you if any problems crop up when we're not here. In the meantime, it looks as though he's coping very well. As his strength builds up, so will his stamina.'

Jamie was driving his quad bike around the circuit by now, following in the wake of his new friend.

'I think I'll go and sit at a table and watch him for a while,' Chloe murmured. 'Thanks for staying with me through today. I'm just planning a quiet evening now, so if you two want to go off and relax, that's fine. You've been more than helpful all day.'

'You're very welcome,' Phoebe said. 'It's

lovely to see him having so much fun. It's hard to imagine that he was so poorly before this.'

'Mr Kirk performed the surgery, didn't he?' Connor asked, and Chloe nodded.

'That's right. He's a brilliant man.'

'That's true.' Connor watched Jamie manoeuvre the bike around obstacles on the course. 'I know he has a long waiting list, especially for the adults on his list, but the advantage of children's surgery is that it can be planned in advance. It works out well when everyone knows the time scale involved and the details of what needs to be done to put things right.'

'Yes, we knew exactly what was going to happen, and Jamie was prepared for everything. It was still worrying, of course, but at least we had time to get our heads around it.'

Chloe went to sit at the tables in the viewing area, and Connor turned to Phoebe. 'Do you have any plans for what you'd like to do this evening? We could wander down by the lake and have a drink at the bar, if you like.'

'That sounds like a good idea. It's warm enough for us to be able to relax outside, isn't it? Perhaps I should go back to the house and change first, though. We've been out and about all day and I'd quite like to just sit for a while.'

They watched Jamie and his friend for a few moments longer, at a distance. Connor seemed to be taken with the gleaming bikes, and there was a smile on his face that prompted Phoebe to say, 'Are you wishing that you could have a go? Quad bikes are the thing these days, aren't they, for men and boys?'

He smiled ruefully. 'I think I've put my racing days behind me. I did enough of that to last me a lifetime in my teens.' He turned away from the circuit. 'Shall we start back to the house? It occurred to me that we could maybe sit out on the balcony and break open a bottle of wine if you'd prefer to do that? We seem to have been walking amongst crowds of people all day, and it might be nice to be peaceful for a while.'

'Okay.'

They walked together along the path to the barn conversion, and once inside the front door Phoebe kicked off her shoes and went upstairs to take a shower. It was good to feel the spray of the water on her face and body, and when she emerged some time later she felt refreshed and ready to face the world again.

Connor must have done the same, because when she went out on to her balcony he was next door, standing by the wrought iron rail, looking out at the landscape beyond.

His hair was damp, gleaming in the evening sunlight, and he had changed into a fresh shirt and casual trousers, so that he looked crisp and clean and wonderfully masculine. His shirt-sleeves were folded back to reveal strong forearms, his skin a soft shade of gold.

She stood for a moment, watching him, taken aback by the sight of him, tall and dark, his long body beautifully lean and perfect in every detail.

After a moment, he must have become aware of her standing there, because he turned and looked at her, his gaze wandering over her from head to toe, his eyes widening.

'You look lovely,' he said. 'Serene and beautiful, like a golden-haired angel.'

'Well, thank you. I feel better for freshening up.' A smile curved her lips. He was looking at her as though he had never seen her before, and that was strange, but at the same time it was oddly uplifting. She was wearing a summer dress, a floaty creation in pastel shades that were dreamy and ultra-feminine, and she liked the way it draped around her, softly touching her curves and drifting on the air with every movement.

He reached for a bottle of wine from an ice bucket on the table and held it aloft. 'Shall we sit out here for a while and watch the sun go down over the horizon? The wine has been chilling for a while, and I've rustled up some nuts and nibbles. It should be just what the doctor ordered.'

She laughed. 'That sounds good to me. Bring it on.'

He pulled out a chair for her and then seated

himself beside her, pouring wine into fluted glasses and handing one of them to her.

'I can see why you used to come here,' he said. 'It wasn't anything to do with the children and the activities, was it? It was more to do with the idyllic setting and the sheer pleasure of sitting back and drinking it all in. Being here, you tend to forget how hectic things are at work, and how rushed we are from day to day.'

She sent him a quick smile. 'I don't know about that. Things have been just as hectic here. We don't seem to have stopped all day. It was so hard to keep up with him, I was beginning to wonder if Jamie actually had a heart problem.'

He chuckled. 'I know what you mean. That boy enjoyed everything so much, it was a joy to see it through his eyes.'

'Like the quad bikes?' She gave him an oblique glance as she sipped her wine. 'No matter what you say, from where I was standing, it looked as though you were getting ready to join him.'

'No, not really. There was a time when I hankered for speed and the adrenaline rush you get from taking risks, but I lost that. I learned my lesson, that if you play wild and heavy, sooner or later you'll end up getting hurt.' He helped himself to nuts from a dish and munched silently, lost in reverie.

'That didn't come about after the time you pranged your father's car, did it? I know you carried on racing for a while after that.'

He nodded. 'I did, but the novelty wore off eventually and I realised that the stunts were becoming more and more dangerous. Some of the older boys from the neighbouring village were coming over in the evenings and began to ramp up the level of excitement.'

She frowned. 'I don't remember much of that.'

'No, you wouldn't. I think your parents had banned you from mixing with me by then and, like a good daughter, you obeyed the rules.' He gave a crooked smile. 'I tried time and again to catch your attention and wheedle you into going off with me on the rampage, but you would never have any of it.'

'That was more to do with the fact that I didn't like the crowd you were mixing with.' She sipped more of the wine. 'As I recall, even Alex was worried about what was going on…and his parents had warned him not to hang around with you, too. Those other boys were out of control, and I made up my mind to steer clear. I remember telling you to do the same, but you didn't want to listen.'

'Yes, I remember that.' His glance moved over her, lingering on the sweep of her cheekbones and the soft line of her mouth, so that a flood of warmth ran along her throat and pooled in her abdomen. Perhaps he noticed the effect he was having on her, because his eyes took on a glimmer of amusement, and he reached for the wine bottle once more. 'I always listened to what you had to say,' he murmured. 'It just took me a while to realise that you were making good sense.' He poured more wine into her glass.

'And when you realised it,' she asked, 'what happened? You moved away from the area when you were eighteen, and I was never quite sure what had brought on the sudden urge to leave. I know you had a major falling out with your mother and father and they were never quite the same after that. Was it to do with the accident down by the quarry?'

He hesitated for a moment before answering. 'Partly. It was inevitable, I suppose.' He put his wineglass to his lips and took a deep swallow. 'Things were getting out of hand. I knew that the lads from the next village were looking for trouble. I'd already started to pull back from the more outrageous stunts, but my friend Matt, who was one of their crowd, was still wrapped up in trying to act the part of a macho man. They'd organised a car race along a stretch of disused road that led to the old quarry, and I was worried that something bad would come of it.'

He slowly twirled the wineglass in his fingers. 'It was doomed from the outset, because the road was full of potholes and there were hairpin bends along the way. Of course, that just made it all the more exciting.'

She stared at him, her hand poised over the plate of cheese straws he'd put out on the table. 'You didn't go there to race with them, though, did you? I could never bring myself to believe the rumours that went flying around afterwards.'

'I followed. Matt was determined to go along, and I was worried. He thought he could take the ringleader on and come out of it unscathed, and nothing I said to him would make any difference.' He pressed his lips together, as though the memory was painful, even after all this time.

Phoebe frowned. 'So Matt went ahead and raced the leader? There were lots of theories and suppositions at the time, but I was convinced that you wouldn't have been foolish enough to take part.'

He nodded, drawing in a shuddery breath. 'I warned him that it was madness to go along with what they were planning. I told him he could end up badly hurt, or worse, but he'd made up his mind, and he wouldn't listen to me. I tried to stop him physically, but he shrugged me off and went after them anyway.'

Phoebe put down her glass. 'I remember reading about it in the local newspaper, about a young man, eighteen years old, who overturned his car into a ditch down by Calder's Cross. He had to be pulled out of the wreckage...' She broke off, staring at him. 'There were whispers around the village about a crowd of lads taking part, but none of that was in the paper.'

'The true story never came out publicly. It all ended so badly that no one wanted to admit that they'd been anywhere near the place.'

Phoebe frowned, thinking back to the time before Connor had gone away. Everyone had pointed the finger at him back then, and she remembered how he had withdrawn into himself, a sullen, rebellious youth lashing out verbally at anyone who had taken him to task.

'I was there,' he said, his voice roughened,

'and I saw it happen. He took a bend too fast, the car flipped over and he finished up on the other side of the road, in the ditch. His car was a mangled wreck.'

His face had paled visibly as he had told her all this, and now she reached for his hand, clasping his fingers as though she would take away the painful memory and draw it into herself.

'What did you do? You must have been horrified.'

He nodded. 'I was in shock. Everyone else disappeared once they took in what had happened. They were out of their minds with dread because he was trapped in the wreckage and they couldn't get him out, and then they realised that big trouble would follow if people found out what had gone on. I think they wanted to help, but they were young and foolish and very scared, and so they drove away.'

'But you didn't?'

He shook his head. 'I called the ambulance and waited with him. I could see that he was bleeding badly from his chest, and I didn't know what to do to help him. I took off my shirt and bundled it up into a pad to make a compress, and held it in place to try to stem the bleeding until the emergency services arrived. I talked to him, doing what I could to keep him conscious and comfort him the best way I knew how. I knew it was bad. I was desperately afraid that he was going to die.'

'You must have been worried sick.' Phoebe ran her hand along his arm in a tender caress, as though she was comforting the youth of all those years ago, the eighteen-year-old who had stayed there and watched his friend's life ebbing away. 'I'm so sorry. It was a terrible thing to happen.'

'It was the worst…and I knew that it was such a waste, such a useless, stupid event, and it was all for nothing but a show of male pride and bravado. I felt sick.' His mouth moved awkwardly as his thoughts roamed back over that awful time. 'The paramedics were fantastic, though. I was so impressed by the way they took charge. They couldn't get him out of there because the firemen needed to cut the wreckage away from him first, but they reached him through the mangled door and the shattered window.'

He gave a small shudder, remembering. 'I didn't think there was any hope for him, but they put a tube in his throat to help him breathe, they gave him fluids to replace the blood he had lost, and all the time they explained to me what they were doing, because I was distraught and scared to death and they recognised that.'

'Did you go with him to the hospital?'

'Yes, but they took him into A and E, and then he went up to Theatre for emergency surgery. He had a bad chest injury as well as fractured limbs and abdominal bleeding. It was touch and go. I wanted to see him when he came back down to Recovery, but he was unconscious and his parents were with him. I wasn't allowed near him again. And then the police wanted to interview me.'

Pain was etched on his face. Phoebe slid out of her chair and knelt down beside him, putting her arms around him. 'I'm so sorry you had to go through all that. I wish I'd been there with you.'

A rough-edged sound rumbled in his throat, a short laugh without humour. 'I'm glad you weren't. You were barely sixteen, a sweet, innocent girl who needed to be shielded from all that. Having you there would just have given me something else to worry about.'

'I was always strong. I would have helped you through it.'

He smiled then, and reached out to stroke her face with a smooth drift of his fingertips along the soft sweep of her cheeks. 'That's what I always found so endearing about you…the way you care so much. You were always calm and centred, and I admired that in you. I would never have put you through that turmoil, though.' He pressed his lips together. 'No one could help me back then. I had to find my way by myself.'

She shook her head. 'Your parents were there for you, surely?'

'No, not exactly.' His mouth made an awkward

twist. 'It didn't happen like that. My father went ballistic when he found out what had happened. He blamed me for Matt's accident. He said I was up to my old tricks, with no thought for the consequences, just running wild and causing trouble for everyone.'

Phoebe frowned. 'But you told him how it was, didn't you? You weren't to blame.'

'He didn't believe me.' He gave a short, ragged laugh. 'It was ironic, really. The police accepted what I said. My car wasn't damaged in any way and there were tyre tracks to show that others had been there, but my father wasn't listening to anyone. We had a huge row, and I moved out of the house. I went to stay with my sister for a while.'

She gasped. 'That's so, so sad. I can't imagine what you must have been feeling.' She reached up and held him, pressing her cheek against his in a warm gesture of compassion, her thoughts overwhelmed by the image of the teenager alone in his desperate plight. 'I knew something had gone dreadfully wrong. I just couldn't see that you had anything to do with the accident.'

'I'm glad you had faith in me, at least.' He wrapped his arms around her, drawing her close to him. 'Matt's parents were beside themselves with grief,' he said. 'They were bewildered and racked with concern in case he didn't pull through. Even if he did, the odds were that he would bear the scars for life, and he might not walk again. It was a dreadful time. I used to go to the hospital and hang about waiting for news, but it took months for him to recover, and his memory of what happened was hazy. When he was well enough, we talked, and he struggled to come to terms with his injuries. He was always such an active person, and to see him in that hospital bed was heartbreaking.'

Phoebe lifted her face to him. 'He pulled through in the end, though, didn't he?'

Connor's mouth curved faintly. 'He did. He still walks with a limp, and he had his spleen removed, so that he's on medication and they have to regularly monitor his white blood count, but he's still around, and able to enjoy life, and in the end that's what counts.'

'I'm so glad.' She smiled and looked into his eyes, and for a moment neither of them spoke.

Connor's gaze travelled over her features, slanting along the smooth line of her brow and moving down over the pink sweep of her cheeks. His glance came to rest on the soft curve of her mouth, and a far-away look came into his eyes, a faint glimmer of light flickering in the grey depths, a look that was full of hidden promise.

He lowered his head towards her and somehow she knew what he was about to do. When he brushed his lips over hers it was as though it was meant to be, and that wonderful moment of completion was a wholesome, breathtaking expression of the bond that had held them together through all the years.

His kiss filled her with sweet sensation, rippling through every part of her body so that each cell was sparked into quivering response, and a fire raged inside her, lighting her up, urging her to cling to him and fuse with him until they were as one.

His hands stroked her, caressing her arms, the gentle curve of her spine, leaving a trail of fire in their wake. She needed him, wanted him, loved the warmth of his body next to hers.

After a while, he drew in a ragged breath. 'I was always afraid to tell you what happened back then,' he murmured, his grey eyes watchful. 'I thought you might think as others did, that I was responsible.'

'No.' She shook her head. 'I wouldn't have done that. I know you would never put anyone else in danger. You were reckless, but only with your own life.'

He hugged her to him once more. 'Thank you for that. It means a lot to me to hear you say it.' He nuzzled her cheek with his own, and then searched for her lips, kissing her again, hungrily, urgently, as though he would make up for all the time they had missed.

Phoebe returned his kisses, wanting this moment to go on for ever. She loved the way his hands moved over her, shaping her slenderness, gliding up over her rib cage to cup the soft swell of her breasts. Her whole body trembled with desire. Being in his arms was all she had ever wanted. Why had she waited so long for this to come about?

But then reality began to creep in and the dreamy, candyfloss world she had imagined began to melt away. This was Connor who was holding her, Connor who charmed all the girls and left a trail of broken hearts behind him.

What was she doing, letting him take over her heart and mind? It was madness to let him see how vulnerable she was, how easily she would fall into his embrace.

Slowly, she eased back from him.

'Phoebe?' He looked at her, sensing a change in her. 'Are you okay?'

'Yes,' she said. 'I'm fine. I just... I don't know if...'

He gave a soft, faint sigh, and lowered his forehead to nestle against hers. 'It's all right,' he said. 'I think I know what's going through your head.' He leaned back and held her for a moment or two at arm's length. 'It's okay. I understand. Things ran away with us and now you're having second thoughts.' His gaze meshed with hers. 'Am I right?'

'Yes,' she whispered. 'I'm sorry.'

CHAPTER EIGHT

'REMIND me some time in the future that you owe me big time for this,' Jessica said, pausing for a moment to lean against a tree and get her breath back. 'A sponsored jog might well be a good way to keep fit and raise money…' she sucked air into her lungs '…but the novelty tends to wear off after the first eight or so miles.'

Phoebe was too busy bending from the waist in an effort to relieve a stitch to be able to answer just then. Instead, she contented herself with nodding. Straightening a moment or two later, she managed, 'Seemed like a good idea at the time.'

Jessica laughed. 'Don't they all?'

Alex came and flopped down on the grass beside them. 'Who's for sharing a cool energy drink?' He held out a flask, and Jessica reached for it, sliding down beside him.

'Oh, yes, please,' she said. 'You're my man. You're everything I ever wanted.'

'Say that to my face instead of ogling the bottle,' Alex complained, holding the flask out of reach. 'You tell all the men the same thing. I heard about you and Connor when he brings you food.'

Jessica chuckled. 'Yes, well, stop being so jealous. I'm dying of thirst.' She slid down on to the grass, putting on her best pleading expression.

Alex gave in, handing over the drink. 'And where is Connor? He was jogging with us not so long ago, but he seems to have disappeared.'

'He dropped behind to stay alongside Lisa from A and E,' Phoebe murmured. It hadn't escaped her that Connor was still on very friendly terms with the woman, and it was vaguely unsettling to know that he wasn't suffering any qualms of unrequited love or anything resembling it after their weekend away.

It was selfish of her to feel that way, she knew

it, but it rankled all the same. Connor had backed off after that kiss, making no attempt to sweet-talk her into his arms once more, and she had tried to convince herself that it was what she wanted.

She was an emotional mess...that was the trouble. She was trying her best not to get involved with him, and anyway her affections were all centred on Alex, weren't they? So why did she feel so thoroughly mixed up?

'And earlier I saw him talking to some man I haven't seen around here before,' Jessica put in. 'Does anyone know who he is?'

'Search me,' Phoebe said, dropping down beside them.

'I think he's someone from the media,' Alex ventured. 'He was supposed to be doing a write-up of the event, or maybe there was going to be something on the TV about it—I'm not quite sure, but anyway Connor was hoping that we would get some publicity and that way draw in more funds for the neonatal unit.'

'You can't fault him, can you?' Jessica said.

'Connor never seems to do things by halves. He's worked hard over the last few weeks to help organise this fun run.' She paused, taking a long swallow of the drink. 'I think he has well and truly upset Mr Kirk, though, because he's still talking about the long waiting lists for cardiac patients. He's trying to persuade my boss to open up the theatres at the weekend, and I think he even spoke to management about it.'

Alex nodded. 'I have the feeling he's going to try to get this media fellow to do a TV programme about changing things in our hospitals. He spoke to management about it, but if the consultants aren't happy I can see him getting himself into deep trouble, one way or another.'

Jessica handed the flask to Phoebe. 'That won't stop Connor. Nothing ever does, once he's made up his mind.'

Phoebe was quiet, thinking things through as she drank the cool liquid. Sometimes, she wondered if Connor still wasn't on a breakneck course, doomed to set himself against everyone in authority. It grieved her to see him at odds with everyone and everything, because deep down she felt he deserved so much better. His instincts were right, but they would always land him in bother of some sort.

'It's true, though, we're overrun with patients down in Cardiology,' Jessica said, leaning back against the tree trunk. 'The outpatient clinics are bursting at the seams, and now one of the consultants has gone off sick we're in even more trouble. There are so many people on waiting lists, it's like a deluge every time we open the doors.'

'Cardiology has always been one of the most pressing specialties,' Phoebe murmured. 'Until we find a foolproof way of preventing heart disease, the health service is always going to be creaking under the strain.'

'Maybe.' Jessica stretched, easing her muscles. 'If you're still wondering what specialty to take up, perhaps you should think about joining us. You're still having doubts about working with children, aren't you?'

'Wouldn't you? It's heart-rending. One of my babies from Neonatal was born with a heart defect and he has to have an operation soon to correct it. He's been really ill, and he isn't putting on any weight or managing to breathe without help.'

Jessica glanced at her. 'This is the baby that Connor referred to you some time back, isn't it? Poor little thing.' She pulled a wry face. 'Mind you, I noticed you said "my babies". That seems to me as if you're already hooked on Neonatal, even if you deny it at every step.'

Phoebe gave a crooked smile. 'It was a slip of the tongue, that's all. I love the babies to bits, but I worry about them all the time, and I don't think my constitution will stand it for much longer. I don't have the same problem with adults, because somehow they don't seem nearly as vulnerable.'

Jessica laughed. 'And we all know that's not true, don't we? You're a hopeless case, Phoebe.' She stood up, getting ready to go on her way. 'I'm off. I want to get to the Riverside Pub and drain them dry of long, ice-cold drinks.' She looked down at Phoebe and Alex. 'Anyone else ready to go?'

Alex groaned, and Phoebe shook her head. 'I need at least ten more minutes.'

'Wimps, the pair of you.' Jessica grinned, jogging on the spot as though she was on a spring. 'See you in half an hour or so.'

'Where does she get her energy from?' Alex pulled a face and shook his head. 'It's beyond me.'

'Unlike the rest of us, she wasn't on the late shift last night.'

Alex rolled onto his back, laying his head on Phoebe's lap. 'That's true. And she wasn't struggling to prepare for an end-of-month case presentation, was she?' He glanced up at her. 'You've been a terrific help to me over these last few weeks, you know. This presentation for my consultant is really important and I don't think I would have managed to get a grip on things without your help.'

'I was glad to do it…especially since the patient you'll be talking about is the mother of the baby we transferred to Somerset.'

He nodded. 'The baby's doing all right, isn't she? I heard she would be coming back here in a few days, which means her mother will be able to be with her.'

'Both of them are doing well by all accounts. It's just the father we have to worry about. He's still being kept under careful observation last I heard. Connor was checking up on him in Intensive Care.'

She was suddenly aware of a long shadow blocking the sunlight from her eyes. She glanced up and saw that Connor had come to join them.

'You two look very cosy,' he remarked, casting a glance from one to the other. 'Will I be interrupting anything if I were to sit down beside you?'

Alex peered up at him. 'Yes, you will. We were just thinking having about a roll in the hay. Go play with Lisa.'

'Can't do that.' Connor sent him a smoke-grey glance. 'She's gone off with my friend John. He's deep into making television programmes about troubleshooting, and she's keen to find out everything there is to know about medicine in the media. I think she's planning on specialising in sports medicine, and apparently he knows a lot of the football celebrities.'

Alex sat up. 'Really?' he said, wide-eyed. 'I think I might go and have a word with him. Where are they?'

'They branched off a couple of minutes ago.' Connor waved a hand towards a footpath that disappeared among the trees. 'It's supposed to be a short-cut.'

Alex was already on his feet. 'I'll see if I can catch up with them,' he said. He glanced at Phoebe. 'I'll catch up with you at the pub. If I'm there first, I'll save us all a table, and we can order lunch.'

He set off along the footpath and Phoebe smiled wryly, shaking her head. 'I sometimes wonder if boys ever grow up.'

Connor came and sat down next to her, resting his arms on his knees. 'Of course we do. We just enjoy slipping back every now and again.' He produced a bottle of water and began to unscrew the top. 'Want some?' he asked.

'Thanks.' Phoebe drank some of the water, and then handed back the bottle. She sent him an oblique glance. 'I heard that you were trying to get publicity for this sponsored jog,' she said. 'Thank you for that. We've had so much interest already, and because of that we're going to be able to add a sizeable amount to the neonatal fund. It means that a lot of babies will benefit.'

'I was hoping that would be the case. I know how much these little ones mean to you.' His gaze rested on her. 'Have you given any more thought to working with children on a permanent basis?'

'I'm still not sure,' she murmured, 'though I did wonder about specialising in Cardiology...not so much with children, but in general.'

He smiled. 'I can understand that. It's a branch of medicine that's interested me more and more lately.'

She looked at him in surprise. 'I thought you

were set on working in A and E? Has that changed?'

He was thoughtful for a while. 'It's not so much that I want to work in Cardiology, but more to do with the fact that I see a lot of cardiac patients coming into A and E. Most of them are on waiting lists for surgery, but their condition changes while they're waiting for it to happen. It isn't anyone's fault, but the system's bursting at the seams. I'd like to be able to do something about that, either by helping to bring about a change in waiting times or by emphasising preventative measures. I suppose I could do that by writing articles for papers and magazines.'

She studied him for a moment or two, taking in the strong line of his jaw, the straight nose, his beautifully formed mouth. Perhaps it was unwise of her to do that, though. It brought back so many memories of the way he had kissed her, and a small thrill of yearning ran through her. She didn't want to feel this way about him, but just being near him was enough to plunge her body into sensory alert.

'I still have trouble taking it in that you've changed so much over the years,' she murmured. 'It must have been such a big step for you to go from being a wild, unbridled teenager to immersing yourself in medicine. What was it that made you decide to become a doctor? Was it your friend Matt, and the terrible thing that happened to him?'

'Yes, it was definitely that. I went from seeing no hope for him to witnessing a miracle. The paramedics, doctors and nurses—everyone played their part in putting him back together. I was so impressed by the way they did their jobs. They were utterly professional, and yet it was clear to see that they cared. They brought him back from the brink and gave him his life back.' He gazed at her, a smile forming on his mouth. 'Seeing that gave me a new purpose in life. I knew that I had to do something worthwhile.'

'But you had left home,' Phoebe said. 'You said that there was a big row with your father. Did he relent and put you through medical school?'

He shook his head. 'I kept in touch with my parents, and let them know where I was and what I was doing… I wanted to let my mother know that I loved her and had no problem with her, but I wouldn't ask my father for anything, on principle.'

She frowned, shooting him a quick glance. 'Was he the reason you rebelled so much as a boy? You always seem to have been at odds with him.'

'I guess it was. I didn't realise it at the time, of course, but he never seemed to be around when I needed him. He was out of the country a lot, running his business, and when he was home he didn't always have the time or the patience to listen to me. I know he was under pressure, and I suppose I made things worse because I went off the rails, wanting him to notice me.'

She cupped her hand, covering her eyes to shield them from the sun. 'But your mother was there for you, wasn't she? Didn't that smooth things over for you?'

'Not really.' His mouth made a wry shape. 'She wasn't happy a lot of the time. She didn't like him being away so much, and she retreated into a world of her own for a while. Then she pulled through that and made a life for herself, taking up new interests. Of course, when Olivia married and had children she became a doting grandmother.'

'It seems strange that we knew nothing about what was going on.' Phoebe thought back to the village life and the big house where Connor and his family had lived. 'We all thought you had a golden existence. It just shows that you can never know what goes on behind closed doors, doesn't it?'

'I guess it does.'

'So, if you weren't getting on with your father and you weren't prepared to ask for help from the family, how did you manage to fend for yourself?'

Connor started to pick at a blade of grass. 'I found work in the City. In fact, for a while I did a couple of jobs, one in the daytime and another in the evening. It was hard, but I managed to get some savings behind me, and it gave me the start I needed. Then I applied to medical school and they were willing to give me a place.'

He reached for the water bottle, tipping back his head and putting it to his mouth. His long fingers curved around the neck, and then he began to swallow, and Phoebe watched the movement of his throat in fascination.

He finished drinking and offered her the bottle once more, looking at her with a quizzical expression. Phoebe realised with a small start that she'd been staring, but she hurriedly pulled herself together and nodded.

'Thanks.' She put out a hand to take it from him, and for a second or two their fingers touched, tangling momentarily, sending a shock wave of heat through her entire body. For a brief flash of time she contemplated tipping the water over her hot face, but she came to her senses and drank slowly, letting the water cool her.

She made to hand the bottle back to him, but it slipped a little before her fingers steadied it once more and a few drops of the liquid trickled down her throat and along the creamy swell of her breasts, exposed by the scooped neckline of the top she was wearing.

Connor's gaze followed the trail of glistening droplets, and a soft smile touched his lips. 'Do you want me to brush that away for you?' he asked, his voice deceptively serene, completely at odds with the gleam in his grey eyes.

'I'm sure I'll manage,' she told him, a wave of heat washing over her.

'Oh, that's a shame,' he murmured. 'It would have been no trouble at all.'

'You were telling me about medical school,' she said, thrusting the bottle into his hands and fixing him with a warning blue glance. 'It can't have been easy for you, and yet you seem to have done well for yourself. I should imagine your mother must be proud of you.'

'She says so.' His mouth curved. 'As to doing well, I suppose that's subjective. I took advice from a friend in the City, and made a few investments, and I supplemented my income by writing a few medical articles for newspapers and magazines. They were keen on having the student's viewpoint, along with real-life stories about my experiences along the way.'

He studied her, letting his glance wander over the burnished gold of her hair, and the slender line of her body, neatly clad in jeans and cotton top. 'It seems strange, doesn't it, that you, me and Alex have all followed the same path?'

'Perhaps that's why we're friends, because we all think much the same way. For myself, it was because Emily made such a big impression on me that I wanted to be a doctor. Alex has always been interested in medicine. It runs in his family.'

'Yes, of course. His father's a GP. I remember his father used to take the time to talk to me and I found myself wishing that he was my dad. He seemed to understand so much. After all, we were related, and it wouldn't have been much of a stretch to ask him to adopt me.' Connor grinned.

He looked around. 'We had a good turnout today for the jog, didn't we? I guess everybody is going to meet up at the pub. Maybe we should be on our way and join them?'

Phoebe nodded. She watched him stand up, unfurling his long body with supple ease. He held out a hand to her and she took it, letting him pull her to her feet.

Only he didn't let her go once she was upright. He held her, his arm sliding around her waist, and for a moment he simply stood, looking down at her, drawing her up against his taut masculine frame, so that every part of her began to tingle in heated awareness.

His grey gaze wandered over her face, as though he was drinking in her features, and slid down to follow the creamy line of her throat, lingering on the soft swell of her breasts. He bent his head towards her, as though he would rest his head against hers, but at the last moment he turned, his glance lingering on the full curve of her mouth. She was sure he was going to kiss her, and for a heady moment she wondered if she should allow herself the taste of forbidden fruit.

He was everything she should avoid. All her instincts told her that she should turn away from him, but he was pure temptation, tantalising her with everything about him that was ultra-masculine, thrilling and made her weak at the knees.

He remained completely still, his whole body poised, as though he was waiting for her to give the slightest hint that this was what she wanted, but as she hovered on the edge of acquiescence, the sound of voices in the distance floated on the air.

She took a step backwards. 'You're right,' she said. 'We've stayed here longer than I expected, and the others will be waiting for us. Alex said he would save us a table.'

'Ah, yes…Alex,' Connor murmured. 'I'd almost forgotten about him.' He held her for a moment longer, and then reluctantly released her. 'That wouldn't do at all, would it?'

CHAPTER NINE

'THEY want us down in A and E,' Katie said, replacing the phone on its base. 'A baby is coming in by ambulance—her GP called to say that she's concerned because she detected a heart murmur.'

'Do we know whether there was a congenital defect at birth?' Phoebe was checking lab forms, but now she looked up.

Katie nodded. 'She was born prematurely, and initially she was diagnosed with a heart defect—patent ductus arteriosus.' She frowned. 'I've come across that before—it's a blood vessel that allows blood to bypass the lungs while the baby is in the womb, isn't it?'

'Yes, it is. Usually it closes within the first

hours of life after the baby takes its first breath and the lungs became active.'

'Hmm. Well, that didn't happen in this instance,' Katie said. 'Apparently she was given medication to help it along, but it seems that it wasn't effective. The consultant believed that the defect would resolve itself as the baby grew, and the decision was made to discharge her from hospital after a few weeks. Of course they arranged to follow up on her progress at regular intervals.'

'That's the usual procedure,' Phoebe commented as she put her lab forms to one side, 'but obviously things have gone wrong with this baby.'

Katie frowned. 'So, if the ductus arteriosus stays open, oxygen-rich blood is returned from the heart to the lungs instead of being circulated around the body, and this causes increased pressure in the lungs' main artery.'

'That's right,' Phoebe murmured. 'And in turn this might bring about a build-up of fluid in the lungs, putting a strain on the heart.' She glanced at Katie. 'What symptoms does she have?'

'Her heart rate is very fast. The parents reported that she looks unwell—she's short of breath, breathing fast, and she's very pale. There's also some wheezing in the chest.'

'That doesn't sound too good, does it? It could be the beginnings of congestive heart failure, or there again it could be a respiratory infection causing the trouble—or both.' She frowned. 'Okay, I'll ask the senior house officer to take over here.' Phoebe mentally readied herself to go and tackle this new emergency. 'How long before they get here?'

'Around fifteen minutes.'

'All right.' Phoebe was already on her way to the door. 'We'll set up a twelve-lead ECG as soon as she arrives, and we'll need to organise an echocardiograph to see what's going on with the heart.'

Katie hurried along beside her to the lift. 'Okay, I can see to all that.'

Once they were down in A and E, Phoebe hurried to Reception. 'Has the baby arrived yet?' she asked the clerk. 'I'm looking for Rachel Morgan.'

The girl shook her head. 'Not yet. She should be here any moment now.'

'I'll go and wait for her, then, at the ambulance bay,' Phoebe murmured, glancing at Katie.

Katie nodded. 'I'll shoot off to Resus.'

Over in the ambulance bay, Phoebe discovered that Connor was waiting by the emergency entrance doors. He was talking to his friend John, the man who had gone along with them on the sponsored jog.

'Hi, Phoebe,' Connor said, throwing her a quick smile. 'We don't see you down here all that much, do we? Not as often as I'd like, anyway. Are you waiting for a patient or have you come especially to see me?' He came to slide an arm around her waist, putting on a blatantly hopeful expression, and despite the tension that had been mounting in her since the call about the baby, Phoebe's mouth softened.

'Sorry to disappoint you,' she murmured, her lips curving. 'I'm here for a patient…a baby girl.'

He wrinkled his nose in mock disappointment,

letting his hand fall from her waist. 'Me, too…only mine's a male adult.'

Phoebe missed that arm around her. It was as though she came to life when he held her, as though he poured new energy into her veins and revitalised her whole body, and now she was left with a sense of loss.

He gestured towards his friend and then said, 'You remember John, from the other day, don't you?'

Phoebe nodded towards the young man. 'You were hoping to interview people from the hospital, weren't you? Didn't you say you were planning some sort of TV programme?'

'That's right.' John nodded enthusiastically. 'The hospital chiefs have agreed that I can do a kind of troubleshooting documentary. They're proud of their record here, so they have nothing to worry about, but the idea behind the programme is that we outline the way the health service can be improved—by choosing to concentrate on one particular hospital, we can show

how things work at the moment, and how they might be made to work better.' He shot a quick glance at Connor. 'It's all his idea, of course, but my bosses were all for it.'

'I can imagine that they were.' She wasn't so sure that all of the consultants would be happy to entertain the idea, but Connor was obviously determined to make his mark, one way or another. She didn't know whether to admire him or succumb to exasperation for the way he persisted in setting the cat among the pigeons.

An ambulance siren sounded in the distance, and Phoebe immediately stiffened, getting ready to receive her young patient.

'Are you okay?' Connor asked, noting Phoebe's sudden pallor. 'Are you worried about the baby that's coming in?'

She frowned. 'It's not that I'm worried… I mean, of course I am, in a way…but I have to psych myself up every time I treat these little people. I'm always on edge because they're so tiny and vulnerable and just starting out on life and so much depends on what we do here. I can't seem to get used to it. It never gets any easier. I must have used up more of my reserves of adrenaline since I've been in the neonatal unit than I have in any other department in the hospital.'

Connor smiled wryly. 'That's because it means so much to you…but it doesn't do to live on your nerves. There comes a time when you reach breaking point, unless you do something to change things beforehand.'

'You're probably right.' It occurred to her that John was listening in, and now she looked at him and said quickly, 'I hope you're not going to write this down or record it in any way. This is just peculiar to me, and it's not something that I want to share with everyone and his neighbour.'

John lifted a hand in denial. 'I don't work that way,' he said. 'I'll always ask your permission first. Anyway, I can understand how you feel. I'm like that with any kind of medicine—that's why I stick to journalism and the media.' He grinned.

'The trouble is,' Connor murmured, letting his

glance drift over her, 'you care too much. It colours your judgement and tends to make you apprehensive because you think that so much depends on you and how you act. In fact, without you and all the people on your team, the babies in your care would probably not have much of a chance at all. You're the reason they survive and go on to thrive. Those that don't make it are usually the ones that are born too many weeks premature, and their chances as a whole weren't very great to begin with.'

She thought about that for a moment. A lot of what he said made sense to her. It was this feeling that everything depended on her actions that had always made her doubtful about working with these babies. It was an awesome responsibility.

The ambulance pulled into the bay, and now Connor was on the alert and looking to see if this was his patient who had arrived. It wasn't, though, and Phoebe moved forward to assess the infant that the paramedics wheeled out of the vehicle.

She saw that there was a faint blue tinge to the baby's lips, but she was already being given oxygen, and so she quickly checked the monitors. 'We'll take her straight to Resus,' she said, guiding the paramedics to the paediatric bay. She gave a quick, backward glance at Connor, but he was already moving to meet his own patient. The bond was cut, and she was feeling the loss already.

The paramedics completed the handover and went back to their vehicle to take their next call. Phoebe began to examine the baby.

'The doctor's right about the heart murmur,' she told Katie a short time later. 'We'll do an echocardiogram and we need to call for a consultation with Mr Kirk.'

'Okay. I'll set things up. Will it be all right if the parents come in here when they arrive? They should be along shortly, and I expect they'll want to be with her.'

Phoebe was checking the ECG readout, and realised with a feeling of apprehension that the baby's condition was worsening rapidly. 'Yes, that will be fine.' She frowned. 'They need to know what's going on… But you should warn them that when they see her she'll be on a ventilator to support her lungs. I'm going to put the tube in her throat now, and connect her to the machine. Perhaps you could sit with them, give them a cup of tea and talk to them about what's happened to her before you bring them in here?'

'I will.' Katie was sad, looking at the infant. 'It's not looking promising, is it? I expect Mr Kirk will want to operate.'

Phoebe nodded. 'Judging by her collapse, I think you're right.'

By the time the baby's parents came into the room some time later, and stood, waiting anxiously just a few feet away, Phoebe had completed the procedure and the baby's echocardiograph had been done.

She was conscious of them watching her every move, and she glanced towards them, saying, 'Rachel was having trouble with her breathing because of fluid collecting in her lungs. I'm giving her medication to help relieve the congestion, and the machine is supporting her breathing. I think you'll find she'll be much more comfortable soon.'

The baby's mother was watching the monitors, and she said, 'Our family doctor said that there might be a problem with her heart. What will happen to her? We knew things weren't quite right when she was born, but we thought she would grow out of it, and yet now it looks as though everything's gone badly wrong.'

'It's possible that she has a chest infection that has put her body under stress and made things worse,' Phoebe said. 'The lab will test for that, but I'm giving her antibiotics to try to clear it up, just in case.'

She gave the parents a reassuring smile. 'It's worrying for you to see your baby like this, I know, but these complications do happen from time to time, and there is surgery she can have that will correct it if necessary. Mr Kirk, the consultant, is coming to take a look at her, and he'll be able to advise you more about what can be done.'

'Surgery? What kind of surgery?' the baby's father asked. 'We were hoping that it wouldn't be necessary.'

'It's quite possible that it won't…but usually, when the ductus arteriosus doesn't close on its own, and the baby becomes ill because of it, it's better if things are corrected surgically. It doesn't mean that she'll need open-heart surgery, or anything like that. There is a procedure that is much less invasive, where the surgeon can close up the defect, by inserting a catheter into the blood vessel and putting a plug in place.'

Rachel's mother was clearly anxious, but she was watching her baby closely and she said, 'She looks quite peaceful, doesn't she? Much better than she was earlier.'

'Yes, she does. It looks as though the medicine's beginning to take effect.'

The baby moved then, her arms lifting, trembling slightly with the exertion, before gliding back into place. 'I think she was having a bit of a stretch,' Phoebe said, smiling. 'I know it's hard, but try not to worry. Mr Kirk is very skilled, and he'll know what's best.'

'Thank you.'

Phoebe left them to sit with the baby for a while. 'I'll go and take another look at the results of the echocardiograph,' she told Katie. 'Bleep me if there are any problems, will you?'

Katie nodded, and Phoebe went along to the doctors' workstation, set up in a small bay where the computers were available for them to check results. She typed in the heading that would bring up the file she wanted, and while she was waiting for it to load, she swivelled around on her seat, peering out into the central area.

Connor was emerging from one of the resuscitation bays, and her heart gave a little flip in her chest at the sight of him, before it struck her that he seemed preoccupied, his features taut and his whole demeanour tense.

'Are you okay?' she asked.

He looked across the central space towards her, and his face relaxed. 'Of course,' he said, coming over to her. 'I'm just concerned about my patient. He's only forty years old, with a young family, and he's had a major heart attack…the second in a year…and things are not working out well for him. I've performed all the interventions I'm able to at the moment, and now I'm waiting to see if I can get him on the list for emergency surgery.'

'No wonder you look as though all the hounds are after you. It's never easy, with a backlog of patients, trying to sort out who has the highest priority.' She sent him a quick, concerned look. 'You're not doing battle with Mr Kirk over this, are you? I don't believe he's operating today.'

Connor shook his head. 'No, but my patient is on his waiting list…has been for nearly a year. He won't survive another heart attack—he may not even come through this one.'

'I'm sorry.' She reached out and touched his arm. 'You tell me that I should be confident and not worry, but you go through the wringer just the same as I do, don't you?'

'It's not quite the same.' He gave a brief smile. 'I know it's not my fault if anything bad happens. I do everything I can to put things right, but sometimes the system seems to work against me, and that can be frustrating, to say the least.'

She studied him thoughtfully for a moment or two. Somehow, she couldn't help but respect him for the energy and drive that made him what he was. 'You'll never sit back and simply accept the way things are, will you?'

'Probably not,' he said, looking into her eyes as though he would see into her soul. 'And that goes for you and the way you try to steer clear of my radar as well,' he murmured. 'You know I have you in my sights, don't you? I think you're gorgeous and everything that's perfect all rolled up into one. I don't know why you keep backing away from me.'

She gave a rueful smile. 'Maybe it has something to do with the way you constantly stir things up all around you. I need peace and quiet in my life…someone calm, to smooth my path and make me feel good about things.'

'I could do that…I think,' he murmured, spoiling the effect by looking doubtful. 'Well, occasionally, at any rate. Like at the barbecue this evening. I guarantee to show you a good time. All the kebabs you can eat, crisp, sparkling wine, plenty of that, and pleasant surroundings… They say the Quayside Pub is the place to be of a summer's evening.'

She laughed. 'Well, considering that I organised the whole venture, I'd say that's rich. And as to showing me a good time, I dare say you promise that to all the girls.'

His brows shot up. 'Which girls?'

'Lisa, for instance…from A and E? Don't imagine we don't all know about you helping her to move into her new place.' It still bothered her that he had gone to Lisa's new house and hadn't come home at all that night. She tried not to think about it, but it slid through the cracks in her armour and pierced her flesh.

'Ah,' he said on a gloomy note, 'I'd forgotten about the chitter-chatter that goes on around here.' Then he brightened a little. 'Anyway, there's nothing to say that I can't help you move house, is there?' A gleam came into his eyes. 'I was planning on getting a place of my own at some point. How about if you were to move in with me?'

Phoebe shook her head, a smile touching her mouth. 'You're impossible,' she said. 'How can I ever take you seriously? You flit from one bright light to another like a demented moth. Go and see to your patient. He needs you.'

'And so will you, one of these days.' He swooped to kiss her firmly on the mouth, and while Phoebe stared at him in tingling shock, he straightened and started to move away. 'Mark my words, you'll wonder why you ever resisted.'

He walked back towards the treatment bay and disappeared into the room. Phoebe watched him in stunned surprise, her mouth still bearing the imprint of that devilish kiss, while her body was fizzing out of control.

How did he manage to do this to her? She tried her best not to let him get to her, and then he crashed through all the barriers she had put up, demolishing them as though they were nothing more than a house of cards.

Why did she react to him this way? Had he crept into her heart little by little, and taken it over, so that now all she could think of was him? Was this love that she felt for him? Why did it hurt so much?

She tried to pull herself together and turned her attention to the work in hand, bringing up the baby's echocardiograph on screen. Mr Kirk would want to look at this before deciding what treatment to pursue.

'Phoebe, my dear, there you are. Katie said I would find you here.' Mr Kirk came into the annexe, a tall man, distinguished looking, with hair that was showing streaks of grey at the temples. His blue eyes were lit with warmth as he walked towards her.

'You were looking for me?' Phoebe was flustered for a moment. 'Has something happened with the baby?' She checked her pager. 'No one called me.'

'No, no…the baby is stable at the moment. We'll admit her to Neonatology and I'll keep an eye on her from there.' He looked at the echocardiograph on screen, checking the working of the baby's heart.

'See, there's the problem,' he murmured, pointing a finger at the image on the monitor. 'I'm going to schedule her for a catheterisation just as soon as we have the optimum time… within the month, I would imagine. I'm actually on my way to do a ward round, and I thought I would let you know that I'm very pleased with the way you handled things and managed to soothe the parents. It can be very unsettling when these tiny infants come into hospital in acute distress, but you coped very well. Just as you did with the baby boy who was suffering from congestive heart failure some time ago. You brought him along nicely, so that he's doing well now. You and Jessica both seem to share that light touch. Well done.'

'Thank you for that.' She smiled at him, her eyes widening a little. Praise from the consultant was like nectar to a bee, and she was happy to drink it up.

She was in a cheerful mood when she went back to check on the baby once more. 'I've sorted out all the paperwork,' she told Katie, 'so we can go ahead and transfer her over to Neonatology right away. Do the parents know that they can stay with her?'

'They do. It's all arranged.'

'That's good. I'll see her settled in on the ward and then I can go off duty in a good frame of mind.' She frowned. 'Somehow, it seems to have been a long day.'

'A lot of emotional trauma, maybe?' Katie said, sending her an assessing glance.

'Yes, you could be right there.' Phoebe acknowledged what Katie was saying but, then, the nurse was talking about the baby, wasn't she? She herself, on the other hand, thought her problems had more to do with a certain A and E doctor whose grey gaze had the power to send a thrill of response rippling through her nervous system from head to toe.

How was she going to cope with being near him at the barbecue this evening? He only had to look at her and she melted, and that would not do at all.

Still, it was all arranged and, since she was the chief instigator of the event, she didn't really have a choice but to go along.

The pub was crowded with people when she arrived there that evening, but the majority of them were congregated outside by the quayside on the river estuary.

Phoebe went to sample the food that was on offer and found that Jessica was looking at the various tables that had been set up in the open air.

'Wow. There are some seriously good raffle prizes here, Phoebe.' Jessica's eyes widened as she surveyed the table that had been laid out with various gift packages in the courtyard of the Quayside Pub. 'How did you manage to come up with all these? I mean, a flat-panel TV, a luxury hamper filled with goodies, a case of wine—I have my eye on that—and a weekend away for two at a country hotel. They're fabulous.'

Phoebe smiled. 'They are pretty good, aren't they? I approached various companies and asked if they would help out with the neonatal fund. I said we were hoping to collect enough money for an extra bay in the unit, so that we could treat more babies. We have the space available, just not the equipment and so on.'

'And they obliged?'

Phoebe nodded. 'They were happy to do whatever they could. Of course, it helped that Connor's friend, John, was doing a piece for the local paper. That way, they were able to adver-tise their products alongside the article.'

'The whole thing's been a success from start to finish, hasn't it?' Jessica moved over to the grill, where food was being prepared. The appetising smell of burgers, sausages and chicken drum-sticks filled the air. 'Have you tried those kebabs?' she murmured. 'They're yummy…full of mushrooms and peppers and spicy meat.'

Phoebe laughed. 'Something tells me you're hungry again. How come you never put on an ounce of weight?' She helped herself to chicken and kebabs, and then added savoury rice and salad to her plate.

'We're all hungry,' Connor said, coming to join them by the table. His plate was already loaded with food, but he eyed up the breadsticks and added one to the feast. His gaze roamed over Phoebe, gliding over the soft cotton top that outlined her curves and shifting to travel over the jeans that faithfully moulded her legs. Phoebe felt a rush of warmth flow through her.

'She's not part of the feast,' Jessica said in a light-hearted tone, and Connor grinned.

'Shame.' He started to munch on a pizza slice, savouring it and then swallowing slowly as though he was tasting a small slice of heaven.

'You've done really well, Phoebe,' he said. 'You must be well on the way to reaching your target for the fund.'

'We are. I'm really pleased with the way things have gone but, then again, everyone has been so helpful, and we've had a really good turnout, both for the jog and for the barbecue.'

'That's because there's nothing people like better than to get together for food and a glass of something or other,' Katie put in, coming over to the grill. 'The pub is heaving at the seams. As for the raffle, like Jessica said, there are some really good prizes.'

'I'll second that.' Connor was looking at Phoebe, and now he indicated a table a few yards away by the water's edge. 'Shall we go and sit down?'

Phoebe finished adding food to her plate and went with him. Jessica and Katie stayed by the buffet table, chatting about the new neonatal bay that they were hoping to bring into being.

'I thought the weekend away sounded like fun,' Connor murmured, waiting while Phoebe seated herself before coming to sit opposite her. 'Do you fancy a few days in a country hotel?'

'With you?' she asked. Unbidden, her heart-beat slipped into a hectic, jerky rhythm. He was in a playful, good-natured mood, and she knew better than to take him seriously, but her nervous system was taking a while to catch on.

'Of course with me,' he said, his brows lifting in astonishment. 'Who else would you be thinking of taking along? Don't tell me you had Alex in mind...he's really not right for you, you know.'

It was Phoebe's turn to raise her brows. He was joking, of course, but she would go along with him for a while. 'Are you sure about that? I thought he had pretty much everything going for him...he's calm, unflappable, always easygoing. He thinks the world of me.'

'Me, too. I think the world of you.' He looked as though she had injured his sensibilities in some way.

'Really? The thing is, Alex doesn't stir things

up or make waves in any way, whereas you tend to do it on a regular basis.'

'No, honestly, I'm a reformed character. I'm done with trouble. I'm even thinking about putting down roots.'

'Are you?' Suddenly, this didn't seem like a game any longer, and she was curious enough to want to know if he was actually serious. 'I thought you said that you hadn't decided what specialty you wanted to study yet, and that you might be moving away at some point? Has that changed?'

'Well, it occurred to me that I could specialise just as well in this area, the South West. My family all live around here, and I have the feeling that it would be good to come back to my birthplace. I was thinking of buying a house locally…of course, a lot would depend on which hospital I eventually settle in.'

'So you weren't really joking this morning when you talked about moving house?' Her mind did a small somersault at the thought. Hadn't he invited her to move in with him?

'No, I wasn't really joking.' His grey gaze rested on her. 'It crossed my mind that I'd like a place of my own.'

'Are you tired of sharing?' She didn't want to read too much into what he was saying. He confused her, made her mind jump in all directions, and she wanted to be clear about what he was really thinking. 'I suppose it can be a problem sometimes, living with friends. You never really have your own space, and there's always someone else using the kitchen, or else you have to think twice about playing music in the living room when other people want to be quiet.'

He filled his glass with punch from a jug on the table and then took a long swallow. 'That wouldn't necessarily bother me, especially if it was you who was sharing with me. I wasn't being entirely flippant this morning.' A smile touched his mouth.

Her eyes grew wide, and this time her heart didn't mess about with funny little dance rhythms, but instead went into full-scale gallop.

It took her a moment or two before she could get her breath back enough to answer him.

'I never quite know whether or not you're teasing me,' she murmured.

'But you do know how I feel about you, don't you?' His grey eyes were warm and enticing, inviting her to agree with him. 'You brighten up my day whenever you're around, and if I run into you at work it's as though the sun has come out.'

Funny, but that was just how she had been feeling. She gazed at him in wonder, uncertain whether she could take that leap in the dark and let him know just how much she felt for him in return. Would it be too much of a risk to tell him that she wished the two of them could share something, too?

'Hey, babe, I've been looking for you.' Alex appeared by her side without warning, and looked down at her, a wide smile on his mouth. 'I wanted to tell you about the presentation. It went really well, and my boss was stunned. He said he hadn't expected such a clear, concise reading of the nature of the patient's problem, and I obviously had a grasp of all the intricacies of the case.' He beamed at her. 'It's all down to you, Phoebe, for helping me get a handle on things. I love you, babe.'

Phoebe was still trying to cope with all the emotions Connor had stirred up in her, and it took all she had to drag her mind over to Alex. She knew that this meant an awful lot to him, though, and she did her best to share his enthusiasm.

'I'm really pleased for you, Alex,' she murmured. 'You've worked hard. You deserve it.'

'But I couldn't have done it without you.' He leaned down towards her and planted a kiss directly on her mouth, a thorough, purposeful and passionate kiss that said 'Thank you' and 'I'm grateful' and 'You're the best'.

Then he straightened up, and Phoebe looked at him with an expression of bemusement on her face. He smiled, and turned to Connor, starting to tell him all about the presentation.

Phoebe wasn't sure exactly what she felt right

then. She was in something of a state of shock, because this was Alex who had kissed her…Alex, who she had worshipped from afar for so many years. She had even entertained the thought that she might be in love with him, and yet his kiss, coming out of the blue like that, meant absolutely nothing to her.

It was a revelation to her after all this time, that she felt nothing in response, no spark, no feeling of wonderment, no desperate need to have him do that again.

And yet with Connor, there were all of those things and more. She just wanted to be with Connor, to have him near, to have him talk to her, to feel the touch of his hand on her arm.

And it all should have been so perfect, because Connor was telling her that he wanted to have her by his side, to share his life, to share his house… Wasn't that everything that she wanted to hear?

And yet that was precisely where the trouble lay, because in all that there had been no mention at all of any kind of commitment. He was proposing that they would live together, but Phoebe knew that it was nowhere near enough. She needed much more than that from him.

She glanced across the table. Alex was talking, but although he was listening, Connor's gaze was fixed on her, and his expression was one that she couldn't begin to fathom. There was no smile, no look that said he wanted her and could not bear to be without her. Instead, his jaw was rigid, his mouth held in a straight line. Was he disturbed because Alex had kissed her? She hadn't invited the kiss, but perhaps that made no difference to the way he felt about it.

'I heard that they were about to draw the raffle any minute,' Alex said. 'Who's doing that? Will you be the one picking the numbers, Phoebe?'

She shook her head. 'No, my boss is going to do it. Since she runs the neonatal unit, I thought it best to ask her.' She didn't move for a moment, trying to get herself together, but then she said, 'I'd better go and organise things. Excuse me.'

She stood up, walking over to the far side of

the courtyard, where her boss was talking to Katie. For a while, she joined them in chatting about the events of the evening, and then after a minute or so she looked over to where Connor had been sitting.

Only he was no longer there. He was standing by the water's edge, deep in conversation with Lisa from A and E, his arm resting lightly around her waist.

She stared at them, a sick feeling gathering inside her.

CHAPTER TEN

'DID I cause a problem for you with Connor last night?' Alex asked. 'Only I might have been a bit carried away with the results of the case presentation. I wanted to tell you about it straight away. It was only afterwards that I realised that I might have been interrupting something.'

Phoebe looked up from the notes she was studying, and sent him a thoughtful glance. 'I had no idea that you ever realised what was going on around you,' she said with a whimsical smile. 'You always seem to be such a man of the moment, jumping in and tackling things as they come about, without thinking too deeply about any of it.'

He shrugged. 'I generally aim to take life as it

comes…otherwise I might get hung up on things, and to my way of thinking, what's the point in worrying? It might never happen.'

She chuckled. 'That seems a sound enough reason.' Then, more seriously, she added, 'No, there was no problem. I'm sure it didn't bother Connor much at all. Why would it? He doesn't seem to have any difficulty finding other girls to soothe away his troubles at short notice.'

She was still sore about him turning right away to seek out the company of the senior house officer.

'I'm not so certain about that,' Alex said with a frown. 'This thing with Lisa, it may not be all it seems, you know. They work together, so they're bound to be chatty and at ease with one another. Going around together outside work doesn't have to mean anything.'

He stopped suddenly and looked at her, watching her expression change. 'Perhaps I should shut up. I'm making things worse, aren't I?' His mouth turned down at the corners.

She replaced the folder in the wire tray on the desk. Even Alex had picked up on Connor's friendship with the woman.

'You don't have to pacify me, Alex,' she murmured. 'I'm all grown up. I can deal with things all by myself.' Connor hadn't denied any involvement with her, had he, so maybe she wasn't wrong in jumping to conclusions?

Alex winced. 'I know that Connor thinks the world of you. He always has.'

'And I've always thought the world of you.' She studied him musingly. 'I wasn't sure if you'd noticed, or whether you were hoping I would cool off, given time.'

He smiled. 'I knew you weren't really sure about your feelings for me, one way or the other, and I was so deeply involved in trying to get my grades, I wasn't going to push it. And then Connor came along, and I could see which way the wind was blowing.' He pulled in a long breath. 'The thing is, we've always been a bit like family, haven't we, you and I? For some reason,

I always wanted to look after you, and I think it was because I thought perhaps I was in love with you. But then I began to realise that I had feelings for someone else.'

Phoebe's eyes widened. 'You do?' She was stunned by this news. 'Why didn't I know about this?'

He winced. 'Because I felt foolish, and I didn't want anyone to know, least of all her. She doesn't even acknowledge that I exist half the time, and for the rest, she has a very low opinion of me. So I plan to keep my feelings to myself. I do have some pride, you know.' He tried to look non-chalant, but failed miserably.

Phoebe was staring at him. 'But I've never seen you even looking at another woman. As far as I know, the only woman in your life apart from me is…' She broke off, clapping a hand to her mouth. 'Oh, my…are you saying it's Jessica that you're interested in?'

'I'm not saying anything,' Alex said, his voice gruff. 'And whatever I've said to you, I've said

in confidence, because I trust you as though…'
His voice trailed off.

'As though I were your sister,' Phoebe said, shaking her head. 'It all makes sense now. I wonder why I didn't see it?'

Alex picked a file out of the tray. 'Maybe you were too busy thinking about Connor. You and he are made for each other, anyone can see that, only neither of you seems to be able to get over the hurdle of the past. It keeps rearing its head, so that you think he's always going to mess up or fly the coop, and he thinks that you only have eyes for me.'

She let her gaze drift over him. She was astonished by his revelations. 'You know, Alex, it seems to me that you ought to have studied psychology. You seem to understand other people very well, and it looks as though you can see things that others miss. Perhaps you ought to put your insight to the test and have a heart to heart with Jessica. You might be surprised at what comes of it.'

'Did I hear my name mentioned?' Jessica came over to the desk and started hunting for a file. 'I hope nobody is planning on giving me a job to do, because I'm up to my eyes. Mr Kirk's planning to sit in on the case conference—he wants to follow up on recent patients with cardiac problems who have turned up in A and E.'

'We were just saying that you're a good listener,' Phoebe murmured. 'Alex is trying to get on the good side of his consultant, and the case presentation was just a beginning. I think you'd be a great help to him if you were to go through some of the patients' notes with him. You've already done your orthopaedic rotation, haven't you? It might be a good idea if you and he were to get together some time.'

Alex was looking horrified by Phoebe's intervention, and trying to warn her off by making wild signals with his hands and mouth, but Jessica was too busy thinking things through to take any notice.

'That could actually work two ways,' Jessica

said, pondering the idea. 'I didn't do too badly in Orthopaedics, but I'm finding Cardiology quite difficult.' She glanced at Alex. 'Maybe you could help me out with that?'

'Um…yeah, sure…any time,' Alex said, blinking, his body jerking a little in surprise. 'I had no idea you were struggling.' He frowned. 'You should have said.'

'As if I'd do that.' Jessica's tone was scornful. 'Your dad's a GP—I thought he kept you topped up with information so that you were nigh on invincible. I thought you had a problem with ortho because you were too busy taking time out and enjoying other things to be able to keep up with your studies.'

Alex rolled his eyes heavenward. 'I wish…I wish.'

Phoebe could well imagine what he was wishing for, but she didn't stay to hear any more. She left the two of them and went in search of her patient.

Connor was in the case review room, flicking

through a pile of X-ray films that went along with patients' notes, but he looked up as she passed by, and said, 'Hi, Phoebe. Are you sitting in on the follow-up meeting?'

She shook her head. 'I'm expecting a patient to arrive in the next few minutes.' Her glance shifted over him. 'You look as though things haven't been going too well. Is there a problem?' She slid into a seat beside him. When the ambulance arrived with the baby, the siren would alert her.

'I'm concerned about the man who was admitted yesterday—the forty-year-old with the young family. I did everything I could for him—morphine, oxygen, nitro and aspirin. Then I put him on thrombolytic therapy to try to reduce the size of the blood clot and buy him some time. What he really needs is surgery, to remove the clot and put a stent in place to keep the artery open. I still don't know if he'll end up with a decent quality of life. It all depends on how much of the heart muscle was damaged after this second attack. I just feel that if the waiting lists for surgery weren't so long, problems like this could be avoided.'

'You can't put the world to rights overnight,' she murmured, laying her hand on his. 'Anyway, there are other factors to take into account, like preventative measures, diet, exercise, cutting out smoking, and so on. For the rest of it, you do the best you can, and that's all any of us can do.'

'Maybe.' His mouth flattened, and she could see he wasn't convinced.

She changed tack. 'I saw your friend John earlier, going from one person to another in A and E, doing interviews. Is he gathering material for his TV programme?'

Connor nodded. 'He tried to talk to Mr Kirk, but the man wasn't best pleased. He said there was no way he was going to be interviewed on TV, and while there might well be a long waiting list for surgery, he was doing everything possible to clear it, but he wasn't Superman.' He gave a wry smile. 'I think John went away with a flea in his ear.'

'Oh, dear. That doesn't bode well for the case review this morning, does it? I'll be with you in mind, if not in body.'

She squeezed his hand, and he covered her fingers with his palm, giving her a warm, sexy smile. 'I like the bit about the body,' he murmured, looking her over. 'Shall we make a date for later? Say lunchtime, around one o'clock?' Then he frowned. 'Or will you be too busy with Alex?'

Her mouth twisted in a wry shape. 'Like I said before, you're incorrigible, totally beyond help. And as to Alex, I wasn't expecting him to kiss me, you know. He took me totally by surprise.' She paused momentarily. 'Though I can't say the same for you and Lisa, can I? You knew what you were doing when you went and put your arm around her.'

An ambulance siren sounded in the distance, and she stood up, tugging lightly at her hand so that he reluctantly released her.

'That was different,' he murmured. 'And I'm

not a completely hopeless case. You could do a lot to soothe my furrowed brow.' He gave her a puppy-dog look. 'Ditching Alex would be a start. He's never going to swear undying love for you, you know?'

'That had crossed my mind,' she said, beginning to move away. She wasn't going to admit to him that she'd realised some time ago that Alex wasn't the man for her. Neither would she tell him about her conversation with Alex. That way, she might manage to keep a defensive wall in place for a while, at least. 'But that still doesn't mean you're in the running.' She frowned. 'I have to go.'

Hurrying away to meet the ambulance, she thought wistfully about what Connor had said. How deep did his feelings for her really go? Could she trust him to love her and cherish her for the rest of her life?

The baby who had been brought into the hospital was clearly ill. 'He was born prematurely, but was released home a couple of weeks ago,' the paramedic told her. 'His mother says he's floppy and is breathing fast, and hasn't been feeding well. He's also had a couple of episodes of jerking in the last few hours, so I'm guessing he had seizures. His temperature is low at 35 degrees.'

'Thanks. We'll get him into Resuscitation and I'll do a complete work-up.' She glanced at the paramedic. 'Is there anything else I ought to know? Any illness in the family?'

'His brother and sister both have runny noses and are coughing.'

'Okay. I'll keep that in mind.'

As soon as the baby was in Resus, Phoebe began to make a thorough examination. 'I'll have to do blood tests, take a urine sample and send cerebro-spinal fluid to the lab,' she told Katie, who was assisting her. 'There's possibly a viral cause for all this, but I'll get him started on antibiotics anyway, in case there's a bacterial infection. All's not well with his lungs, and it could possibly be pneumonia. We can't run the risk of leaving it until we have the test results back… And we need a chest X-ray.'

Katie was busy preparing the equipment trolley so that Phoebe could carry out the procedures, and some time later Phoebe began to write out the forms that were needed for the laboratory.

'I'm concerned about the seizures,' she said, gazing down at the baby. The child was lethargic, and had a nasal discharge along with his lung problems. 'He's had another one since he's been here, and that means there could be some inflammation of the brain.'

'Are you going to do an EEG?'

'Yes.' Phoebe nodded. 'And we'll need a CT scan of the head. In the meantime, I've started him on medication for the seizures. I'll do a nasal washout, and we'll send that for testing as well.'

A short time later, Katie went to organise the chest X-ray and CT scan, before taking the samples over to the lab.

Phoebe stayed behind and gently stroked the baby's arm. 'I'm so sorry to put you through all that, Ryan,' she said softly, looking down at his tiny, fragile figure, 'but we're doing everything we can to make you better. It's not fair that you should be so ill when you're so little.'

She moved away from the crib, and went to talk to the parents. It was never easy doing that, but she'd learned that if she kept people informed about what was happening to their children, and explained carefully what was going on, the parents were a little easier in their minds.

It would be some time before the test results came back, though, and perhaps it would be sensible to go for her lunch-break now, while things were quiet. She checked her watch. There was a good chance that Connor would be free around about this time, too.

She went to the cafeteria to pick up some sandwiches and coffee before going in search of him.

He was giving medication to a middle-aged man when she stopped by the treatment bay a few minutes later, and she heard him quietly explain to him how it would work.

'Just try to relax,' he murmured. 'This will help

to widen the blood vessels, and you should find that the pain starts to ease off fairly soon.'

He waited a moment, and then said, 'How are you feeling?'

'Better,' the man said cautiously, nodding. 'You were right.'

'That's good. You need to rest now, and the nurse will keep an eye on you. I'll arrange for you to be admitted so that we can see how you go over the next couple of days. We'll need to do some more tests, but they're nothing to worry about.'

He spoke to the nurse for a moment or two, and then came out into the central area where Phoebe was waiting.

'Are you busy,' she asked, 'or do you have time to go for a lunch-break?'

'I should be okay for the next hour,' he said. 'You must have read my mind…or maybe you decided to take me up on my earlier offer?' He sent her a questioning, hopeful glance.

'I don't know about you,' she said, giving him a quelling look, 'but lunch was what I had in mind.'

He grinned. 'Then I guess that goes for me, too.' He started to walk with her out of the emergency department. 'I was thinking I would like to get out of here for a while, maybe go for a walk along by the stream at the back of the hospital. Would you like to do that with me? I know there was a shower of rain earlier, but the sun is out now, and a drop of rain makes everything all the more fresh.'

'Sounds good to me. I was hoping you might be free, so I bought some lunch from the cafeteria…a couple of packs of sandwiches and some coffee.' She showed him her packages. 'I bought enough for two, just in case. I know you like cheese and salad, and there are some Chelsea buns for afters.'

He sent her an appreciative smile. 'If you're trying to win me over for some devious plan that you have in mind, I have to tell you that you're halfway there already.'

'Well, that is good news.' Her lips quirked in a mischievous curve. 'I don't have to worry about signing you up for Mr Kirk's next round of lectures on surgery for chest trauma, then, do I?'

He backed away momentarily, his mouth dropping open. 'You are kidding, aren't you? He's not really arranging a course, is he? Sandwiches or no sandwiches, I don't think I'd want to be doing that for a while. He and I are not exactly seeing eye to eye at the moment.'

'You surprise me,' she murmured, as they walked towards the main doors of the hospital. 'He's an eminent man, and if he was to talk about new procedures in cardiac surgery, he'd be guaranteed a huge audience. Are you really going to let a thing like a small difference of opinion stand in your way? You could learn so much.'

He laughed. 'Okay, so I know that he's the best in his field. And if I was on a cardiology rotation I'd be more than happy to hear what he had to say. Right now, though, it has to be said I'm not flavour of the month with him.'

She shot him a quick look. 'Seriously, I'm sorry to hear that. I know how much it meant to you to get him on your side.'

By now they had crossed the road that skirted

the car park and they started out on the footpath that would take them into the wooded area edging the hospital to one side. Here the shade of the trees lent a cooling effect, and the air was fresh and sweet, inviting them to walk on further.

'There's a clearing in here where we can sit and eat,' Connor told her. 'There's a huge old tree that's been cut down and the trunk makes a perfect bench seat. It should be big enough for us to lay the food packages out as well.'

As he had said, the tree was a perfect place for them to stop and eat lunch. It was dry now, leaving everything brighter, more vivid, the scent of leaves filling the air and mingling with the fragrance of mosses and lichens.

Phoebe set down the packages on the tree trunk and sat down. 'It's beautiful here,' she murmured, looking around and seeing here and there glimpses of colourful flowers, the tiny dog violet, an occasional pink purslane and a small clump of foxgloves.

'That's why I like to come here and just sit for

a while,' Connor said, following her gaze. 'It's very restful.'

He opened a pack of sandwiches and handed it to her. 'How did your morning go?'

She made a wry smile. 'It started off well enough. I managed to cuddle a couple of the babies who were on the road to recovery. There's something really satisfying about being able to hold them and feed them, and watch them suckle hungrily. The baby you admitted from A and E a while back was one of them. He'll be going home soon, and in some ways seeing them well enough to be discharged makes up for all the anxiety.'

He smiled. 'I knew you would love that side of things. I saw how you were with your sister's children years ago. I couldn't help thinking that maybe you would go on to be a paediatrician. I still can't see you doing anything else.'

Phoebe bit into her sandwich. After a moment or two, she said, 'If it was just a matter of holding them in my arms and nurturing them, I would agree with you, but I still have to get over this great hurdle every time a baby comes in suffering from a life-threatening illness. Like this morning… I have to wait for the results of all the tests before I can do any more than give supportive treatment. It grieves me. I hate the waiting. I hate wondering about the outcome every time.'

He studied her thoughtfully for a second or two, and then took a drink from his coffee-cup. 'It's a shame you feel that way. You're such a good doctor, and you should be filled with confidence about what you do. You give so much to these babies. They need you to look out for them.'

'I'm not so sure that I can do it. Perhaps it would be better if I left it to someone else.'

'So you're still thinking about applying for Mr Kirk's team next time?'

'I don't know. Possibly.'

His mouth made an awkward quirk. 'Then you won't want to jeopardise things by helping me out, will you? I was going to ask if you would let John interview you for this TV programme. I thought maybe you would put the case for cutting down operating lists. I've already been interviewed on camera, and said my piece, but the more people we can get to add a positive point of view to the debate, the better chance we have of changing the culture that goes through the hospital.'

She swallowed her coffee, and looked up at him. 'What you really need is Mr Kirk on your side, because if just one of the consultants were to agree with you, the others might consider following suit.' She shook her head. 'The trouble is, I can't see that happening.'

'It isn't going to be easy, that's for sure. Lisa had a word with the consultant she used to work with—Mr Byers—who runs another cardiac team, but even he was sceptical. He agreed to be interviewed, but he isn't going to do anything to further our cause, by the looks of things.'

Phoebe finished off her sandwich and wiped her hands on a serviette. 'You and Lisa are very close, aren't you?' she said on a hesitant note. It bothered her that she was even mentioning it, but the thought of the two of them kept niggling away at the back of her mind and wouldn't leave her alone.

'We get along all right,' Connor said. His gaze narrowed on her. 'Why do you ask?'

Phoebe shrank into herself. 'No reason,' she murmured. 'It was just an observation, that's all.'

He reached for her, placing his hand under her jaw and gently lifting her head so that she had no choice but to look at him. 'It couldn't be that you're just a tiny bit jealous, could it?'

'Do I have anything to be jealous of? I mean, if I were to believe all the things that you've been saying to me, I can't imagine why you're seeing her outside work.'

'Don't you ever go to the pub with colleagues when you've finished your shift? In fact, I know you do, because I've seen you there.'

'That's different.'

His brows shot up. 'How is it different? Explain it to me.'

'I didn't stay overnight at anyone's house afterwards. I wasn't the one who rolled into work wearing the same clothes that I had on the night before.'

Maddeningly, he didn't answer her. Instead, he casually finished off his sandwich and then took a long swallow of his coffee. He reached in the bag for a serviette and wiped his fingers, and then began to clear up all the debris of their lunch, placing it in the bag.

She stared at him. 'Aren't you going to give me an answer?'

His gaze tangled with hers. 'Oh, it was a question, was it? I didn't realise that. I thought you were making a statement of fact.' He tilted his head to one side, studying her, and she had the feeling that he was amused by her frustration. He was teasing her, playing her along.

She turned away from him. 'Forget I said anything at all.'

At last he seemed to relent. 'It's quite true,' he said. 'I did come to work wearing the same clothes as the night before—that wasn't good, and it wasn't something I would normally do, but

I did go and grab a fresh set from my locker so the patients had nothing to worry about.'

Her blue eyes fired sparks at him. 'You're enjoying this, aren't you?'

He laughed, and slid an arm around her shoulders. 'It was all entirely innocent. She had just moved into a new place, and I'd been helping her with taking crates of belongings over there, and so on.'

'I think it's the "and so on" that I'm concerned about. I mean, you wouldn't be arranging furniture or unpacking crates throughout the night, would you?'

His gaze lingered on her testy features. 'You know, I think I'm quite pleased that you're worried about what might have gone on. It makes me think that you might actually care for me a bit more than you've been letting on.'

He tugged her to him, resting his cheek against hers. 'The truth is, I'd finished helping her with the boxes when her new neighbour came round and knocked on the door. The woman said her husband was ill, but she didn't know whether it was serious enough for her to call for an ambulance, and she knew that Lisa was a doctor and wondered if she'd mind taking a look.'

'So you both went round there?'

'We did. Turned out he was having a mini-stroke. We stayed with him, doing what we could for him, and then we waited for the ambulance to arrive. Later, we realised that if the woman went with her husband to the hospital there would be no one to watch over her children who were fast asleep. So I volunteered to stand in until an aunt could come and take over.'

'Oh, I see.' She felt humbled by this revelation.

'Hmm… Do you? Are you sure? Have I managed to restore your faith in me?'

His cheek was nuzzling hers, his lips very close to her own, and she wasn't at all sure that she was in any way capable of thinking logically at that point. It wasn't fair, the way he was distracting her with his warm caresses, letting his hand move over her in tender exploration while his mouth was edging closer to hers.

'I don't…' she began, but she didn't have the chance to finish what she was about to say, because he closed off the words with a slow and achingly thorough kiss, one that sent myriad bubbles of excitement racing through her blood-stream and alerting every fibre of her being.

He took her over completely with that passion-ate kiss. The whole world tilted around her, and all she was conscious of was that wonderful feeling of being folded in his arms, feeling the heavy thud of his heartbeat next to hers, and being overwhelmed by sweet, heady sensations that licked through her body like flame.

She wanted him. More than anything she had ever craved in her life, she wanted this moment to go on and on. She ran her hand over his chest, letting her fingertips trail over the hard wall of his rib cage, smoothing over his velvet skin as though she would absorb every part of him into her memory.

'I need you, Phoebe,' he murmured, brushing his lips across her cheeks, gliding down to leave a path of fire over her throat, and lingering there. 'I don't know why it's taken so long for us to come together. I'm a lost soul without you. I need you to keep me on the straight and narrow.'

'You're asking the impossible,' she whispered. 'You'll always go your own way. Nothing anyone says will ever make any difference.'

He kissed her again, raining kisses over her throat, her cheeks, her mouth. 'It isn't true. I always listen to you.'

His hand stroked the length of her arm, and then shifted direction to smooth over her curves, his palm coming to rest lightly on the fullness of her breast. Her body quivered, loving his touch and wanting more, and when he lowered his head and let his mouth trail over her soft contours, she was lost in a world somewhere between heaven and the bliss of her dreams.

She drew in a ragged breath. 'I wish I could believe you. I wish there was a chance you wouldn't run headlong into trouble at every opportunity.' She let her hands trace the strong muscles of his arms. 'What am I to do with you?'

He lifted his head. 'Accept me as I am?' His grey eyes held a questioning glimmer. 'Take what I have to offer, and maybe we can work the rest out between us.'

She shook her head. 'I wish it was as simple as that, but I've lived on my nerves as far as you're concerned ever since we were young. You were always in trouble of some kind or other, and I wanted so much for things to go right for you. It was agonising, watching you breaking the rules and tempting fate. I always thought you were heading for disaster. Then, when you turned up here, I thought for a while that things might have changed. But I discovered I was wrong about that.' She straightened, easing herself away from him.

He frowned. 'You don't want me to go through with this TV programme, do you?'

'It doesn't matter what I want, does it? I'm afraid

that you're setting yourself up against powerful people—you may have management on your side at the moment, but ultimately you're setting yourself against the consultants, and I can't help feeling that by doing this you're throwing your future away. You have so much promise, so much going for you, and yet you're swimming against the tide, as if none of that matters.'

He sighed. 'I'm sorry that I can't be the person you want me to be,' he said, 'but this is too important to me. People's lives depend on it, and it doesn't matter to me that I'm ruffling a few feathers—I feel that we can achieve something good if we only try.'

He picked up the bag containing the coffee-cups and sandwich cartons. 'We ought to be heading back,' he said. He seemed sad, and Phoebe wanted to reach out and comfort him, but she was battling her own inner demons, and instead she merely nodded and began to walk with him along the woodland path.

CHAPTER ELEVEN

'WE HAVE some of Ryan's results back from the lab,' Katie said, looking across the room to where Phoebe was standing, nursing a baby. The infant lay with his head against her chest and she was gently patting his back, waiting for the soft sound of a burp that would signal a comfortable end to a feed.

'That's good. I'll come and take a look, just as soon as I have my hands free.' Phoebe smiled, placing the baby back in his crib. 'You're doing really well, little one,' she said softly, looking down at him. 'Your mother will be so pleased that she'll be able to take you home.'

Once she was certain that he was comfortably settled, she went over to the neonatal reception desk where Katie was looking through the incoming post.

Phoebe scanned the results. 'The nasopharyngeal washing was positive for respiratory synctial virus,' she said. 'We'll suction his nasal passages and start him on nebulised racemic epinephrine to help open up his airways.'

'Are you keeping him on the on the antiviral medication?' Katie asked.

Phoebe nodded. 'Yes, we should do that until we see what results we have from the blood cultures, and we'll go on with the antibiotics, since the chest X-ray revealed infiltrate on the middle lobe of his lung. He's beginning to respond to the treatment, anyway, so I'm not too worried about him.'

'Okay.' Katie glanced at her. 'You know, I can see a change in you, somehow. You seem much more at ease with what you're doing here. Are you finding that you've adjusted to working with babies now?'

Phoebe nodded. 'I was apprehensive to begin

with, but now I realise that we all have the same worries and anxieties. We go on doing what we can to make them healthy, and the reward for doing that is tremendous. I've decided that I want to go on working in Neonatology.'

'I'm really pleased for you.' Katie gave her a beaming smile. 'When I see you with the babies, I just know that it's the right job for you. I've seen your expression when you cradle them and watch them sucking on their thumbs, and my only worry is that you might decide to keep one of them.'

Phoebe laughed. 'Don't think it hasn't occurred to me.'

She wrote up the instructions in the baby's case notes, and then went to check on her other charges. Baby Rachel was doing well, and hopefully would be having surgery to correct her heart defect within the month, while Sarah, the baby who had been taken to Somerset for special renal care, was back with them in the neonatal unit.

'She's coming on by leaps and bounds, isn't

she?' Katie murmured as Phoebe stopped by Sarah's crib to check on her progress.

'She certainly is. She's beginning to put on weight, and she'll be coming off the ventilator very soon if she keeps this up.' Phoebe gave Katie a smile. 'I can't help thinking that having her mother with her in the unit has helped her along. They were separated to begin with, but the bond between them is very strong. It's as though they've given each other strength.'

Katie nodded. 'Her mother's recovering nicely. Do we know if there's any news of the father?'

Phoebe made a quick check of the monitor and wrote up the medication in Sarah's notes. ' was going to ask Connor about that later today. I know he's been keeping track of how he' doing, but I haven't heard anything more for couple of days.'

In fact, she hadn't seen much of Connor at all and whether that was because he was keeping hi distance or because he was involved in liaisin with the producer of the TV programme, sh didn't know. He had been back to the house they all shared, but he hadn't stayed around for long, and when she had spoken to him he had seemed preoccupied.

It bothered her, this lack of communication, because she couldn't help wondering if he had taken her at her word and was backing away. She wasn't sure what she had expected, but Connor had been part of her life for so long that she was already feeling wretched without him.

'How are things down in A and E?' Katie asked, cutting into her thoughts. 'I heard it was all a bit crazy what with the TV cameras in the corridors and open areas, and the hospital chiefs being interviewed about their thoughts on budgets and targets and all the rest of it.'

Phoebe winced. 'Well, it isn't just to do with A and E. The whole hospital is under scrutiny. So far, management seem to be coming out on top of things with positive views, but John's brought in a troubleshooter to do the bulk of the face-to-face interviews, and he's nobody's fool.

He gets right to the nub of things. I let him do an interview with me on camera, and although it seemed to go all right, it was a nerve-racking experience. I was conscious the whole time that anything I had to say might have repercussions in one area or another.'

'Knowing you, I should imagine you did very well,' Katie murmured. 'You'll have put forward a positive, practical argument. For myself, I've been trying to avoid the whole shebang. If I so much as see a camera I turn around and find another route.' She glanced at Phoebe, frowning. 'Does this mean that you'll be in trouble with Mr Kirk? I know how you feel about this business… you're caught between a rock and a hard place, aren't you? On the one hand you want to keep on the right side of the consultant, and on the other you want to help Connor.'

Phoebe frowned. 'I suppose I'll find out soon enough if there's going to be any backlash. Anyway, I have to go and talk to Mr Kirk about Rachel's surgery. The parents are asking me if I can give them a date for the operation, and it hardly seems fair to keep them waiting, does it? Perhaps I should go and get it over with.'

'Rather you than me.' Katie threw her a rueful smile. 'I'll hold the fort here.'

A short time later, Phoebe took the lift down to the ground floor, and headed towards Mr Kirk's office. There were things preying on her mind, other than the baby's surgery, like how she could help Connor, and whether by setting herself up against a consultant she would be jeopardising her career. This forthcoming chat with Mr Kirk promised to be difficult.

She tapped on the consultant's door and when he acknowledged her, she went in.

'Phoebe,' Mr Kirk said, looking up from his desk, his pen poised in his hand, 'you've caught me in the middle of sorting through my schedule. Sit down.' He waved a hand towards a seat opposite. 'There are so many patients needing attention, every one of them urgent. It's really difficult to work out who has priority.'

She made a rueful smile. 'I hope young Rachel is one of those,' she said quietly. 'As I understand it, the children with this particular heart defect do very well when it's corrected early on.'

He nodded. 'I can give you a date for that...' He flicked through his lists. 'Shall we say two weeks from today?'

'Thank you,' she said. 'The parents will be so relieved.'

They chatted for a while longer, but when she was about to leave, she hesitated.

'Was there something?' he queried.

'It's about the waiting lists—the ones that Connor is worried about.'

He was very still for a moment, looking at her. 'Those lists...yes...well, they are definitely unwieldy and giving me and the patients a lot of grief one way and another. There are so many people suffering from heart problems.'

He sat back in his chair, waiting for her to comment. He tapped his pen abstractedly against the palm of his other hand.

'I've been thinking about that,' she said. 'I've heard in some hospitals it's possible to clear backlogs by involving other members of the surgical team. They do a survey of patients to see which of them are willing to come in over the weekend, and the specialist registrars work with the consultants to decide which cases are the most urgent. Then, over a few weekends, they open up the operating theatres and make big inroads into the waiting lists so that things ease up all round. It doesn't have to be an ongoing process, just a blitz over a period of a few weeks.'

He was silent for a moment. Then he said, 'You and Dr Broughton—Connor—think very much along the same lines, don't you?'

Phoebe sent him an uncertain glance. He couldn't possibly know about her TV interview, could he? The programme wasn't being aired until the day after next. 'I'm not exactly sure about that. Do we?'

'Oh, yes. You see, he put the very same proposition to me just yesterday. In fact, he's been putting it to me on a fairly regular basis. I think he was hoping to wear me down with his persistence.'

'Oh.' She blinked. 'You know, Mr Kirk, it may seem as though Connor is a thorn in your side, but it's only that he's very forward thinking. Most people I speak to say that he's a brilliant doctor. He doesn't want to bring about change for its own sake, but because he feels it will make a big difference to people's lives. He has the best of intentions.'

'Hmm. That was eloquently put, my dear.' His gaze was fixed on her. 'I'll tell you what I told him, shall I?'

Filled with sudden apprehension, Phoebe cautiously nodded. 'Please do.'

He put down his pen. 'I told him that I think it's a workable proposition, especially since he managed to persuade several of the other consultants to join in. He also came up with one or two ideas to ease the hospital budget at the same time. In fact, I put it to my registrar just a short time ago, and he agreed that he would work with the rest of the team to see if they could come up with a plan of action. The same applies to all the other consultants in the cardiology department.'

Phoebe let out a long breath of relief and gave him a wide smile. 'Oh, I'm so pleased to hear you say that. It's wonderful news.' She paused as a thought crossed her mind. 'Of course, a decision like that would go down really well for the TV programme, wouldn't it? What a coup that would be.'

'You could be right.' He was pensive for a moment or two. 'There's something to be said for young upstarts like your friend, Dr Broughton. He's a nuisance, no doubt about it, coming up with ideas that catch us all on the hop…but I have to say he has all the makings of a fine consultant…someday in the not too distant future.'

Phoebe left his office a few minutes later, a smile playing around her mouth. She had been dreading that conversation, and yet it looked as though things would turn out for the best in the end.

Except that she still didn't know if Connor was

at odds with her for her wariness in accepting him just as he was. Would he even give her a chance to let him know that she had thought things through and decided that she wanted to be with him, no matter what the future held?

She was so deep in thought that she would have gone straight by him in the corridor if Connor hadn't put out his arms and walked right up to her, stopping her in mid-stride.

Her body softly collided with his, and she looked up at him dazedly as his arms went around her to steady her.

'Phoebe? Are you okay? You look as though you were miles away.'

'Yes,' she said haltingly, 'I'm fine. I was just on my way back to the neonatal unit.'

'Good. You'll be able to tell Katie that little Sarah's father is out of Intensive Care. She was asking me how he was doing. It looks as though he's on the mend at last.'

'I'm glad about that. We were all worried about him.' Her mind was still foggy from running into him this way, and while he was holding her, it was impossible for her to think straight. Perhaps he read her thoughts, because he released her and took a step backwards, his gaze searching her features in a curious fashion.

'You seem distracted. Is there something on your mind?'

She shook her head. She wasn't going to open up her soul to him when she was still so unsure about what it was he really wanted. He had suggested that she might move in with him, and though he might, in the dim and distant past, have intimated that he loved her, or at least, found her lovable, she couldn't be sure that he really meant what he said.

'I haven't seen much of you these last couple of days,' she said softly, 'and you've hardly said a word to me. I expect you've been up to your eyes in work.'

He nodded. 'That's exactly it. It isn't only the work here in A and E, but I've been following up on my patient who had the heart attack. Mr Kirk operated on him yesterday, and there were a few complications, so I stayed with him to see that he came through it all right. It was a bit scary at first, but it looks as though his heart muscle will recover, and his life will be better than it was before.'

'That's really good news.' She smiled at him. 'You must be pleased.'

'I am. Of course, what with that, and the interviews for the TV programme going on, it's been really hectic.'

He started to walk with her back to the lift bay, and waited with her for the doors to open.

'Are you going back to A and E now?' she asked.

'Yes, but my shift ends in a little while, and then I'm going with John over to the TV studios. They're going to do a run-through of the programme before it airs tomorrow morning.'

She was surprised by that news. 'Is the run-through where they edit things out?'

'That's right. They'll take out anything that isn't needed, and keep the stuff that makes for good television.' He frowned. 'I hope it works out all right. There was a piece about it in the local paper as well as the nationals. There's a lot riding on it—if we manage to get our point across, it could help to change things across the country.'

She smiled, and just then the lift doors swished open. 'I hope it all works out for you,' she murmured. 'Perhaps I'll see you later, back at the house?'

He shook his head. 'Not until tomorrow afternoon, probably. The studios are some distance from here, so I'll be staying at John's house overnight.'

'Oh, I see.' A wave of disappointment washed through her.

He reached out and touched her hair, tucking a golden strand behind her ear and letting his hand rest against her temple. 'I'll say goodbye, then.'

'Yes.' She wanted to lay her cheek against his palm and bathe in his tender embrace, but instead she waited a moment before gathering herself. Perhaps she was hoping that he might lean down and kiss her, but it didn't happen, and so she moved away from him, stepping into the lift.

'Goodbye,' she murmured, as the lift doors closed. Her heart quivered. Already she was missing him.

She went back to Neonatal and passed on the good news to Rachel's parents about their baby's operation, and then she updated Katie on how Sarah's father was doing.

'Connor seems to think he's making an excellent recovery,' she told the nurse. 'That's fantastic, isn't it? That family deserves some good fortune.'

'It's brilliant,' Katie agreed.

Phoebe went off duty later that day, feeling disconsolate because Connor was not going to be around. Jessica and Alex didn't put in an appearance, and she wondered if they were on the late shift, until Jessica rang to say that they were taking time out to go on a canal boat trip.

'We've been working so hard lately,' Jessica said, 'being run ragged in Cardiology and Orthopaedics, and then studying till late in the evening, and Alex thought it would do us good to take a break for a couple of hours. Apparently they run these trips down to the Watermead Inn on a regular basis in the summer months.'

'It sounds like fun,' Phoebe said. 'Enjoy yourselves.'

When Jessica ended the call a short time later, Phoebe wandered disconsolately around the house. Without Connor, she felt as though part of her was missing. How was she ever going to be happy again without him?

She was off duty all the next day, but Jessica and Alex had to go in to work, and so the house seemed unusually empty. She busied herself, tidying up, plumping cushions and generally filling in time, anything rather than sitting and thinking.

The TV programme started midmorning, and she switched on the set, watching avidly. The opening credits came up and what followed was streamlined and professionally put together.

Her own interview passed in a flash, and she was pleased that she had managed to add to the argument for keeping hospital facilities, like operating theatres and pharmacies, available on an almost 24-hour basis.

What surprised her was Connor's TV image. Watching him, she sat bolt upright in her chair, struck by his charismatic, awe-inspiring persona. It was clear to see that here was a consultant in the making, just as Mr Kirk had predicted. People would stand up and take notice of anything that Connor had to say.

'Management has suggested that opening up theatres and running the MRI scanner for longer intervals is going to cost money,' he said, 'but by leasing the outpatient clinics for GP services at the weekend, I'm sure we can cover the expense.'

She switched off the TV and began to pace the room. She was on edge, unsettled, wanting to have him near, but it was still only morning, and she wasn't expecting him back until late afternoon at the earliest. What was there to say that he wouldn't stay on at John's house, enjoying his leisure time with his friend?

Unexpectedly, she heard the sound of a key in the lock of the front door. She frowned. Had Jessica or Alex come back from work for something that had been left behind? Or perhaps it was the landlord, come to make a quick inspection…only usually he gave them notice before he did that.

'I wondered if you would be at home today,' Connor said coming into the living room. 'I was pretty sure that it was your day off.'

Phoebe's heart made a sudden leap. His tall, vital presence seemed to fill the room with new energy. Her spirits lifted. Anything was possible, now that he was home.

'What are you doing here?' she asked. 'I expected that you would still be at John's house. You can't have had time to watch the programme this morning, can you?'

He threw his overnight bag down on to the coffee-table and shrugged out of his jacket, placing it over the back of a chair. 'I saw it on the run-through yesterday. It was first rate, wasn't it?

Even Mr Kirk took part and had something good to say—I rang him to thank him, and he said it was you who put the idea into his head about taking part in the programme. He had been dead against it initially, but since he was going to go along with the whole idea of scything through the operating lists, he said he may as well do the TV bit while he was about it.'

He came over to her and wound his arms around her waist. 'You didn't tell me that you were going to see Mr Kirk and talk to him. You didn't even tell me that you were going to take part in the programme.'

'You were very busy with other things.'

'Yes, I'm sorry about that.' He winced. 'I wanted to come back to you just as soon as I could. I meant it when I said I need you, Phoebe. You're the other half of me. I'm not complete without you. It's always been that way, ever since I can remember.' He kissed her gently, brushing his lips over hers, lingering as though he couldn't bring himself to break off the contact, and

Phoebe felt a sense of elation, as though all was finally right with the world.

She ran her hands over his chest, imprinting the memory of his strong, hard body on the inner workings of her mind. 'Is it true? Do you really feel that way?' It was joyous to hear him say it, but she was having trouble taking it in.

'I do. I mean it. I love you, Phoebe. I've always loved you.' He kissed her again, deeply, passionately, prolonging the moment before he had to break off for air. 'I can change. I can be anything you want me to be, if only you'll say that you love me just a little.'

She moved against him in sheer exhilaration, curling her arms around his neck and tilting her head so that she could feel his lips on hers all over again. 'I love you,' she said, her voice husky with longing. 'I love you just as you are.'

Soft laughter sounded in her throat. 'I know you're never going to change, no matter how you try…you'll always fight for what's right, even if it stirs things up and causes trouble along the way. It's the way you are, and I can't help but love you for it. I tried to back away from it, and I even told myself that Alex was the man for me, but it was a cover, a protective blanket, because in my heart of hearts I knew there was never anyone else for me but you.'

'Wow.' His eyes were gleaming as he looked down at her. 'You've just made me the happiest man alive.' He folded her into his arms, hugging her close, kissing her as though he would never let her go.

Phoebe was in a state of absolute bliss. Everything in the world she had ever wanted was here, now, and nothing could ever make her feel as happy as she was at this moment.

Only just then a mobile phone began to ring, and even though she tried to ignore its insistent tone, it kept on ringing.

Connor gave a heavy sigh and reluctantly eased himself back from her. 'They're not going to go away, are they? Why would anyone be ringing me now? I'm not on duty.'

'Perhaps it's Jessica, or Alex. They're at the hospital, but they would probably be having lunch around now.'

He shook his head. 'It's not likely to be them. I drove by the hospital on my way here, and saw them walking together on the perimeter of the hospital.' His mouth curved. 'They were holding hands... I don't think either of them is going to be taking much notice of anyone for a while.'

Phoebe was bubbling over with happiness. 'Oh, that's great news.'

'Yes, it is.' In the meantime, the phone was still ringing, and he went over to the chair and reached into his jacket pocket to bring out his phone. He frowned, looking at the caller display.

'What is it? What's wrong?' Phoebe could see that he was puzzled.

'Nothing. It's my father.' He clicked the 'receive' button, at the same time reaching out to her and drawing her close, wrapping his arm around her.

'Hi, Dad,' he said, 'are you okay?' He listened for a while and then he began to smile.

'Yes, it was good, wasn't it? I wasn't sure whether or not you would watch the programme. No, it's all worked out really well. They're going to put everything into practice as soon as possible.' He listened again and then laughed softly. 'You could be right. I've already been advised to take my specialist exams in A and E. It looks as though that's what I'll be doing.'

Phoebe looked up at him, an inquisitive look on her face. 'My boss wants me to apply for the post of specialist registrar,' he told her. Then he turned his attention back to his father. 'No, Dad. I wasn't talking to myself. There's someone very special here with me. I was just about to ask her if she would marry me, but your call cut in on us.'

There was a longish silence, and Phoebe stared at him in astonishment, hardly daring to believe what he had just said, but conscious of a flare of excitement racing through her veins.

Connor nodded, still talking to his father. 'I will. I'm sure Mum will want to meet her, too. Sunday lunch sounds fine. I'll check with Phoebe.'

He sent her a smiling glance, raising a brow in query, and she nodded, wide eyed. Sunday lunch? He wanted to marry her? Exhilaration fizzed through her entire body. 'Yes, to both of those,' she murmured, and he smiled broadly and broke off to kiss her long and hard.

'Sorry, Dad,' he said a moment or two later. 'What was that you were saying? Yes, that's right. I think she just accepted my proposal. In fact, I'd better ring off now and find out for sure. See you both on Sunday.'

He ended the call and slid the phone back into his jacket pocket.

'Now, where were we?' He moved to take her in his arms once more, but she laid her palms lightly on his chest.

'Hold on a minute. That was your father? Is everything all right with you and him now?'

He smiled. 'It looks that way. We've been making cautious circles around one another ever since I left home, but we've both tried to build bridges wherever possible. Then this morning he saw me on TV and he said he wanted to let me know that he was proud of me.' He gave a wry laugh. 'This day has been a long time coming.'

'But now it's arrived.' Her face lit up with happiness. 'We're all proud of you and what you did. Did I tell you Mr Kirk thinks you're consultant material?'

His brows lifted. 'Well, that's something good to know.' He ran his fingers gently over her cheek. 'What I really want to know is what do you think about me.'

She reached up and kissed him firmly on the mouth. 'I think you're wonderful husband material,' she said, and his arms closed around her, his lips claiming hers, so that for a long, long while after that they were wrapped satisfyingly in each other's embrace.

MEDICAL™

Large Print

Titles for the next six months…

February

EMERGENCY: WIFE LOST AND FOUND	Carol Marinelli
A SPECIAL KIND OF FAMILY	Marion Lennox
HOT-SHOT SURGEON, CINDERELLA BRIDE	Alison Roberts
A SUMMER WEDDING AT WILLOWMERE	Abigail Gordon
MIRACLE: TWIN BABIES	Fiona Lowe
THE PLAYBOY DOCTOR CLAIMS HIS BRIDE	Janice Lynn

March

SECRET SHEIKH, SECRET BABY	Carol Marinelli
PREGNANT MIDWIFE: FATHER NEEDED	Fiona McArthur
HIS BABY BOMBSHELL	Jessica Matthews
FOUND: A MOTHER FOR HIS SON	Dianne Drake
THE PLAYBOY DOCTOR'S SURPRISE PROPOSAL	Anne Fraser
HIRED: GP AND WIFE	Judy Campbell

April

ITALIAN DOCTOR, DREAM PROPOSAL	Margaret McDonagh
WANTED: A FATHER FOR HER TWINS	Emily Forbes
BRIDE ON THE CHILDREN'S WARD	Lucy Clark
MARRIAGE REUNITED: BABY ON THE WAY	Sharon Archer
THE REBEL OF PENHALLY BAY	Caroline Anderson
MARRYING THE PLAYBOY DOCTOR	Laura Iding

MILLS & BOON®

MEDICAL™

Large Print

May

COUNTRY MIDWIFE, CHRISTMAS BRIDE	Abigail Gordon
GREEK DOCTOR: ONE MAGICAL CHRISTMAS	Meredith Webber
HER BABY OUT OF THE BLUE	Alison Roberts
A DOCTOR, A NURSE: A CHRISTMAS BABY	Amy Andrews
SPANISH DOCTOR, PREGNANT MIDWIFE	Anne Fraser
EXPECTING A CHRISTMAS MIRACLE	Laura Iding

June

SNOWBOUND: MIRACLE MARRIAGE	Sarah Morgan
CHRISTMAS EVE: DOORSTEP DELIVERY	Sarah Morgan
HOT-SHOT DOC, CHRISTMAS BRIDE	Joanna Neil
CHRISTMAS AT RIVERCUT MANOR	Gill Sanderson
FALLING FOR THE PLAYBOY MILLIONAIRE	Kate Hardy
THE SURGEON'S NEW-YEAR WEDDING WISH	Laura Iding

July

POSH DOC, SOCIETY WEDDING	Joanna Neil
THE DOCTOR'S REBEL KNIGHT	Melanie Milburne
A MOTHER FOR THE ITALIAN'S TWINS	Margaret McDonagh
THEIR BABY SURPRISE	Jennifer Taylor
NEW BOSS, NEW-YEAR BRIDE	Lucy Clark
GREEK DOCTOR CLAIMS HIS BRIDE	Margaret Barker

millsandboon.co.uk Community

Join Us!

e Community is the perfect place to meet and chat to kin-
ed spirits who love books and reading as much as you do,
it it's also the place to:

Get the inside scoop from authors about their latest books

Learn how to write a romance book with advice from our editors

Help us to continue publishing the best in women's fiction

Share your thoughts on the books we publish

Befriend other users

rums: Interact with each other as well as authors, editors
d a whole host of other users worldwide.

ogs: Every registered community member has their own
g to tell the world what they're up to and what's on their
ind.

ok Challenge: We're aiming to read 5,000 books and have
ned forces with The Reading Agency in our
augural Book Challenge.

ofile Page: Showcase yourself and keep a record of your
cent community activity.

ocial Networking: We've added buttons at the end of every
ost to share via digg, Facebook, Google, Yahoo, technorati
d de.licio.us.

www.millsandboon.co.uk